William Shakespeare's
Hamlet

adapted by **Rebecca Dunn**
illustrated by **Ben Dunn**

magic
wagon

visit us at
www.abdopublishing.com

Published by Magic Wagon, a division of the ABDO Publishing Group, 8000 West 78th Street, Edina, Minnesota 55439. Copyright © 2009 by Abdo Consulting Group, Inc. International copyrights reserved in all countries. All rights reserved. No part of this book may be reproduced in any form without written permission from the publisher.
Graphic Planet™ is a trademark and logo of Magic Wagon.

Printed in the United States.

Adapted by Rebecca Dunn
Illustrated by Ben Dunn
Colored by Robby Bevard and Wes Hartman
Edited by Stephanie Hedlund and Rochelle Baltzer
Interior layout and design by Antarctic Press
Cover art by Ben Dunn
Cover design by Neil Klinepier

Library of Congress Cataloging-in-Publication Data

Dunn, Rebecca, 1965-
   William Shakespeare's Hamlet/ adapted by Rebecca Dunn; illustrated by Ben Dunn.
      p. cm. -- (Graphic Shakespeare)
   Summary: Retells, in comic book format, Shakespeare's play about a prince of Denmark who seeks revenge for his father's murder.
   ISBN 978-1-60270-188-5
   1. Graphic novels. [1. Graphic novels. 2. Shakespeare, William, 1564-1616--Adaptations. 3. Youths' writings.] I. Ben Dunn, ill. II. Shakespeare, William, 1564-1616. Hamlet. III. Title. IV. Title: Hamlet.

PZ7.7.D88Wi 2008
741.5'973--dc22
                                                        2008010742

Table of Contents

Cast of Characters

Hamlet
Prince of Denmark

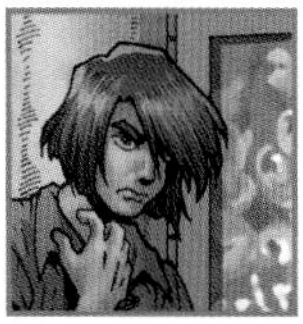

Ophelia
Polonius's daughter

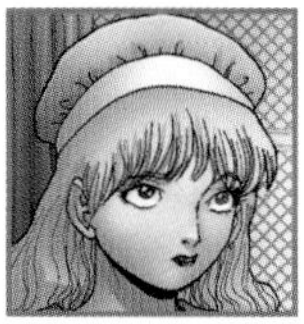

Queen Gertrude
King Hamlet's widow, Hamlet's mother

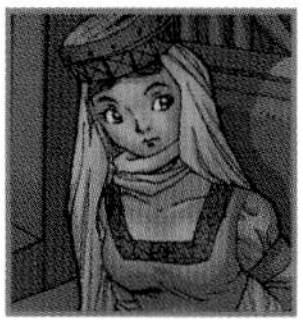

Prince Fortinbras
Prince of Norway

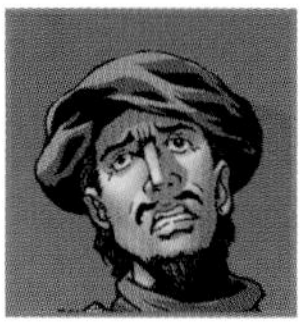

Marcellus
Officer

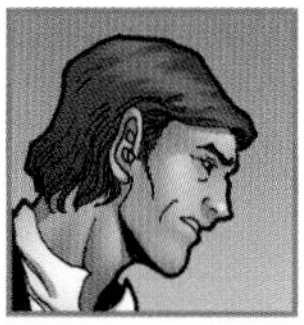

King Claudius
New king of Denmark

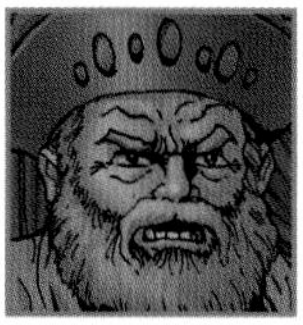

Voltemand
Courtier

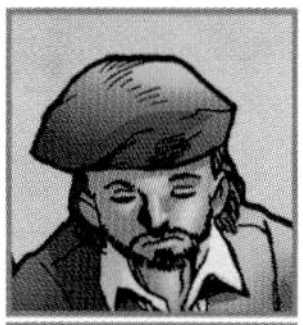

Cornelius
Courtier

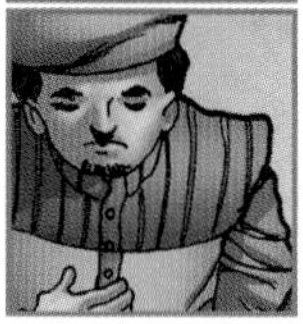

Laertes
Ophelia's brother

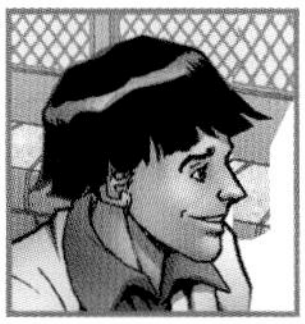

Lord Polonius
Father of Ophelia and Laertes

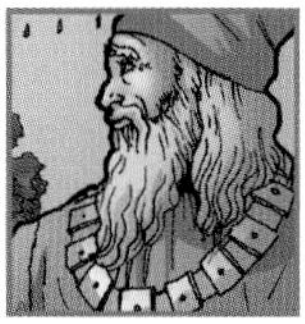

Reynaldo
Lord Polonius's servant

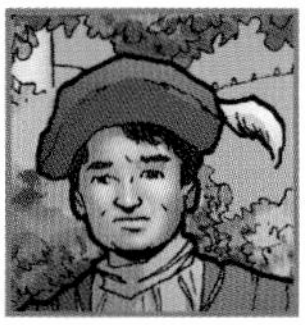

Horatio
Friend of Hamlet

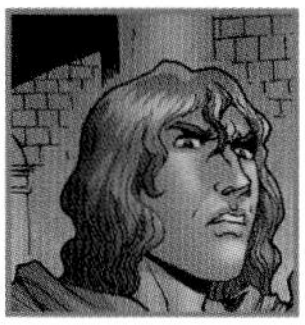

Guildenstern
Courtier

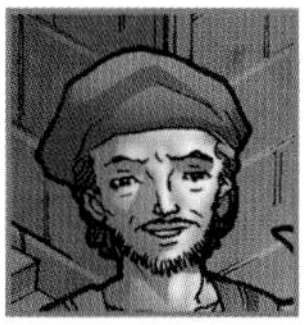

Rosencrantz
Courtier

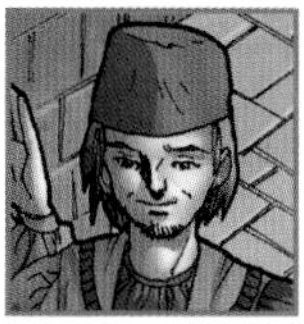

Ghost of Hamlet's Father

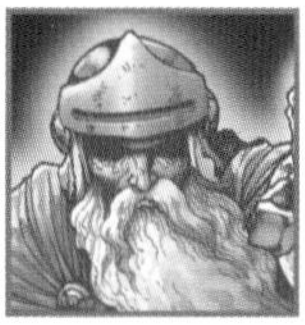

Our Setting

Hamlet is set in Denmark. Denmark is a country the European region of Scandinavia. Most of Denmark is on the peninsula called Jutland and the 400 surrounding islands.

In about 12,000 BC, the first hunters entered the land that is now Denmark. These people brought tools and weapons. Over many centuries, the people improved their tools and began to expand their territory. In the 800s AD, the Vikings took control of the area. They continued to expand the area.

Over time, the Danes fought to take back their country. In 1047, a Danish king held the throne, but years of civil and international war followed. Today, Denmark is working to improve its economy and trade.

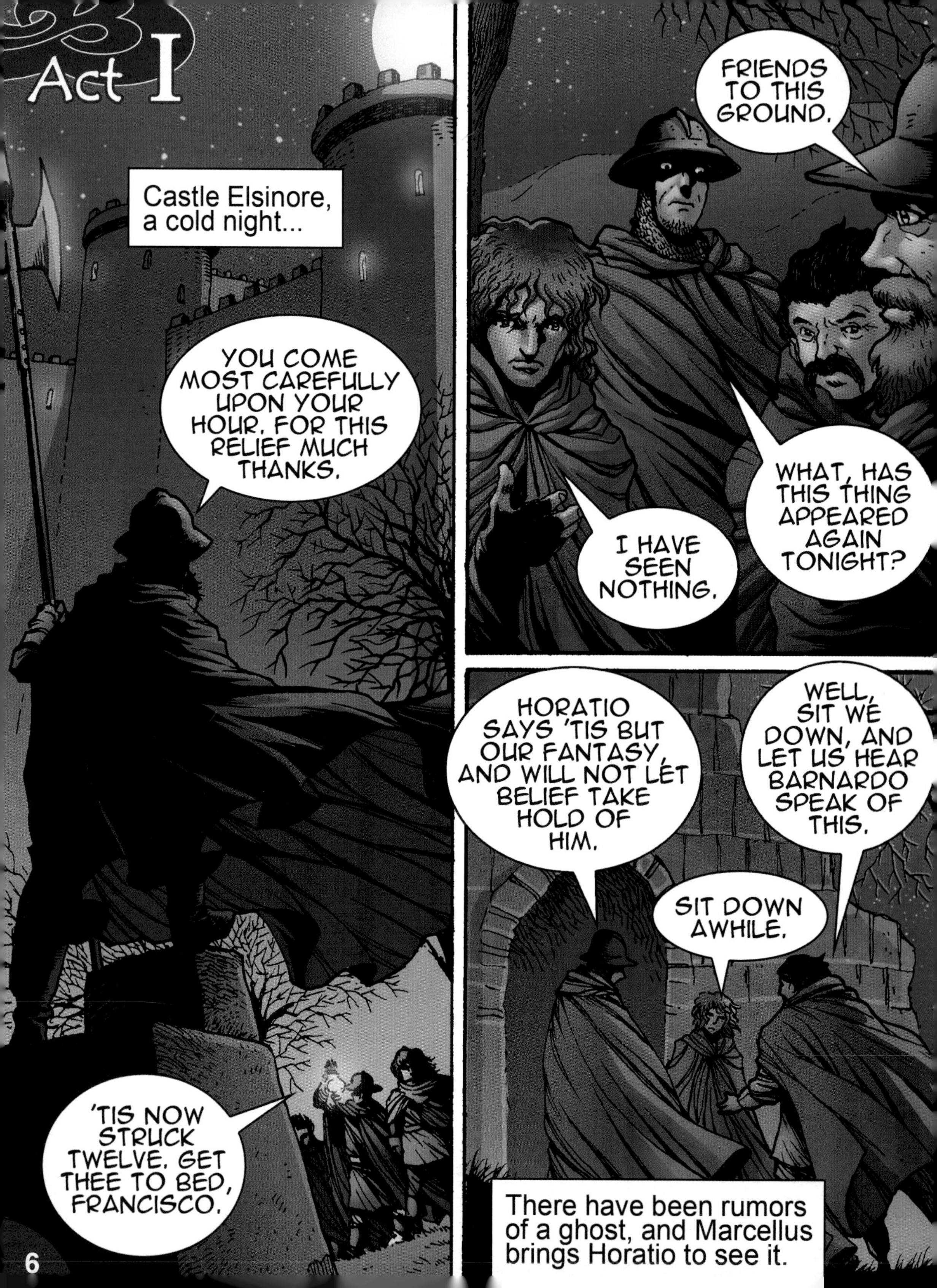
Act I
Castle Elsinore, a cold night...
YOU COME MOST CAREFULLY UPON YOUR HOUR. FOR THIS RELIEF MUCH THANKS.
'TIS NOW STRUCK TWELVE. GET THEE TO BED, FRANCISCO.
FRIENDS TO THIS GROUND.
WHAT, HAS THIS THING APPEARED AGAIN TONIGHT?
I HAVE SEEN NOTHING.
HORATIO SAYS 'TIS BUT OUR FANTASY, AND WILL NOT LET BELIEF TAKE HOLD OF HIM.
WELL, SIT WE DOWN, AND LET US HEAR BARNARDO SPEAK OF THIS.
SIT DOWN AWHILE.
There have been rumors of a ghost, and Marcellus brings Horatio to see it.

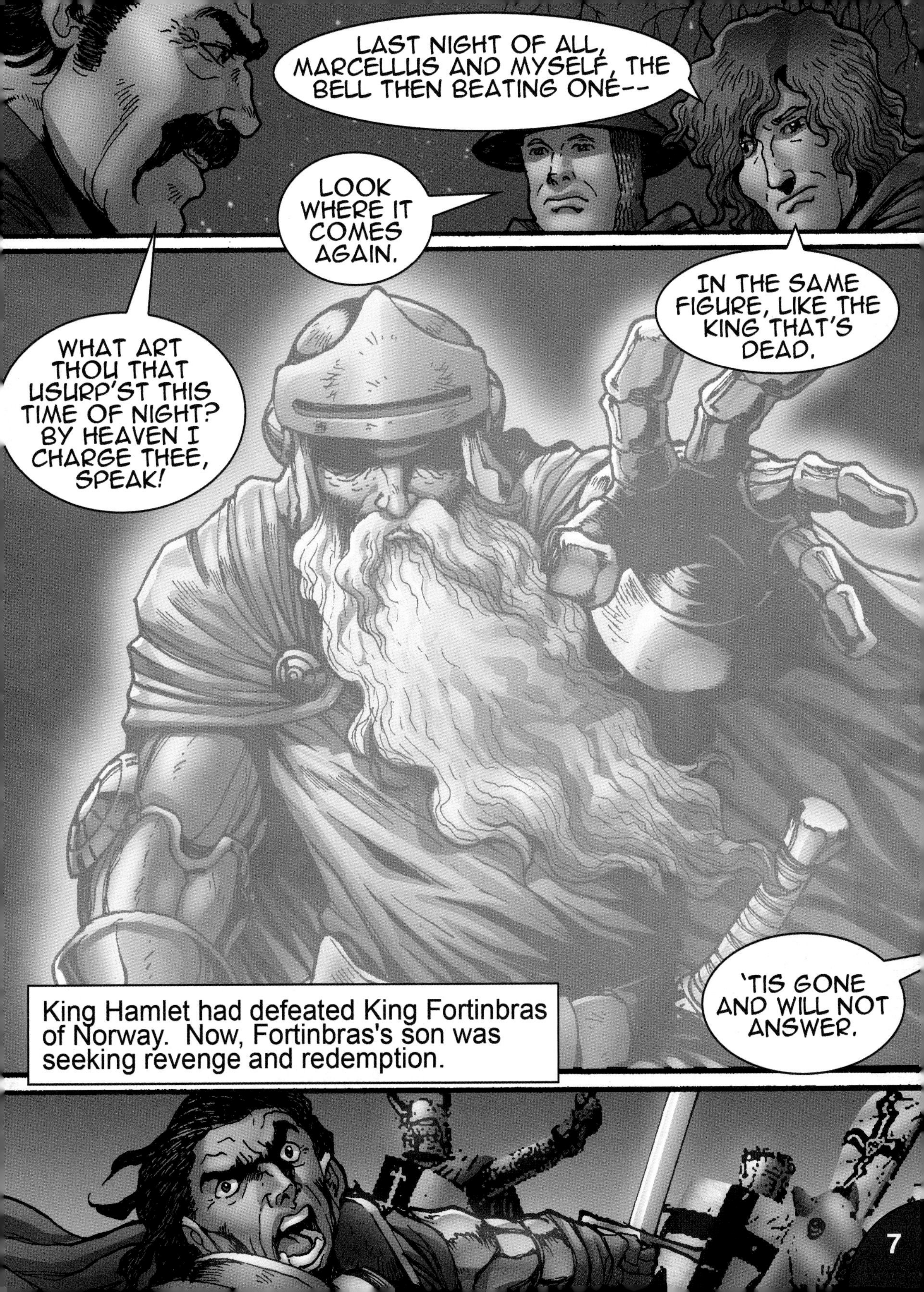

LAST NIGHT OF ALL, MARCELLUS AND MYSELF, THE BELL THEN BEATING ONE--
LOOK WHERE IT COMES AGAIN.
IN THE SAME FIGURE, LIKE THE KING THAT'S DEAD.
WHAT ART THOU THAT USURP'ST THIS TIME OF NIGHT? BY HEAVEN I CHARGE THEE, SPEAK!
King Hamlet had defeated King Fortinbras of Norway. Now, Fortinbras's son was seeking revenge and redemption.
'TIS GONE AND WILL NOT ANSWER.

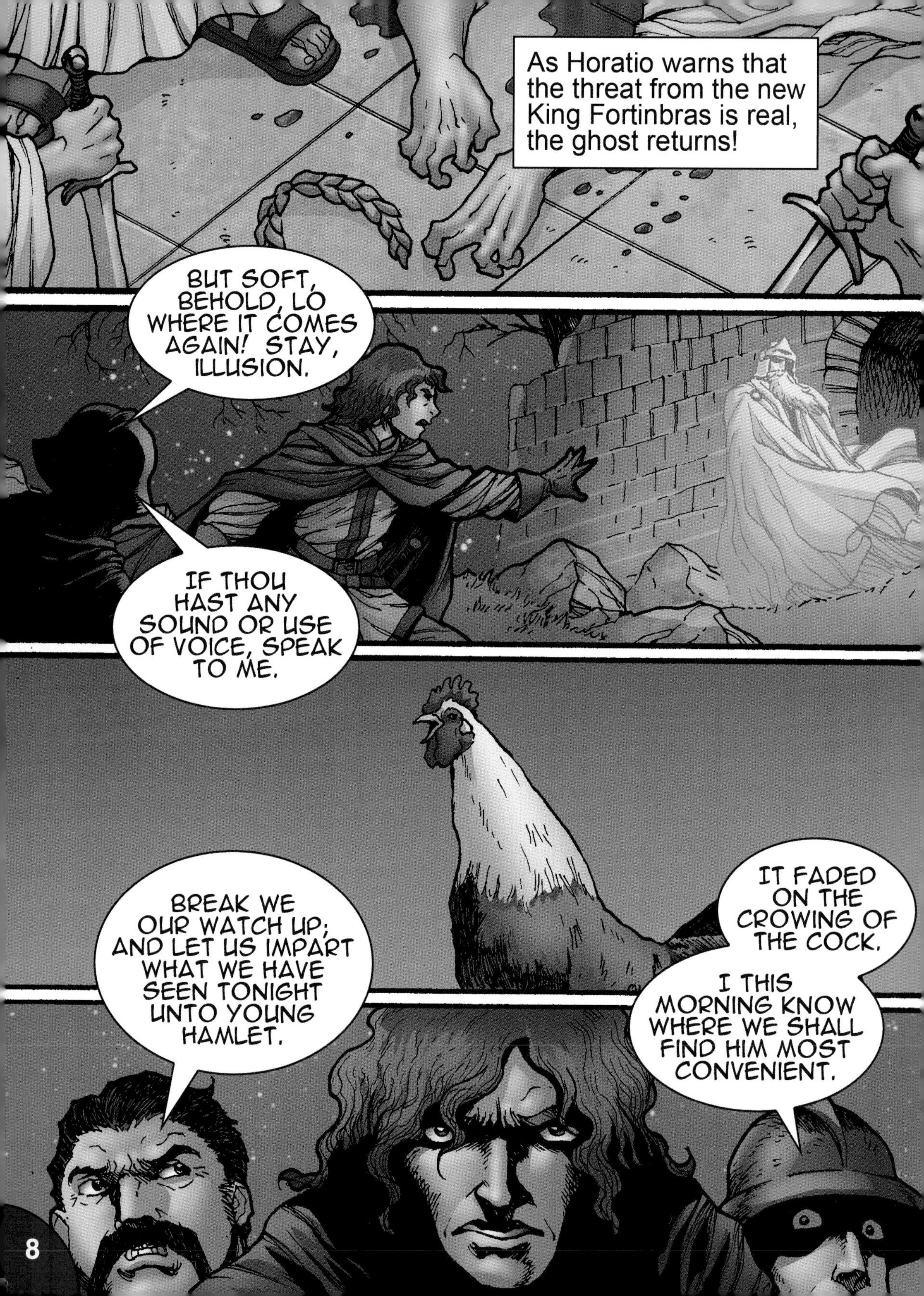
As Horatio warns that the threat from the new King Fortinbras is real, the ghost returns!
BUT SOFT, BEHOLD, LO WHERE IT COMES AGAIN! STAY, ILLUSION.
IF THOU HAST ANY SOUND OR USE OF VOICE, SPEAK TO ME.
IT FADED ON THE CROWING OF THE COCK.
BREAK WE OUR WATCH UP; AND LET US IMPART WHAT WE HAVE SEEN TONIGHT UNTO YOUNG HAMLET.
I THIS MORNING KNOW WHERE WE SHALL FIND HIM MOST CONVENIENT.

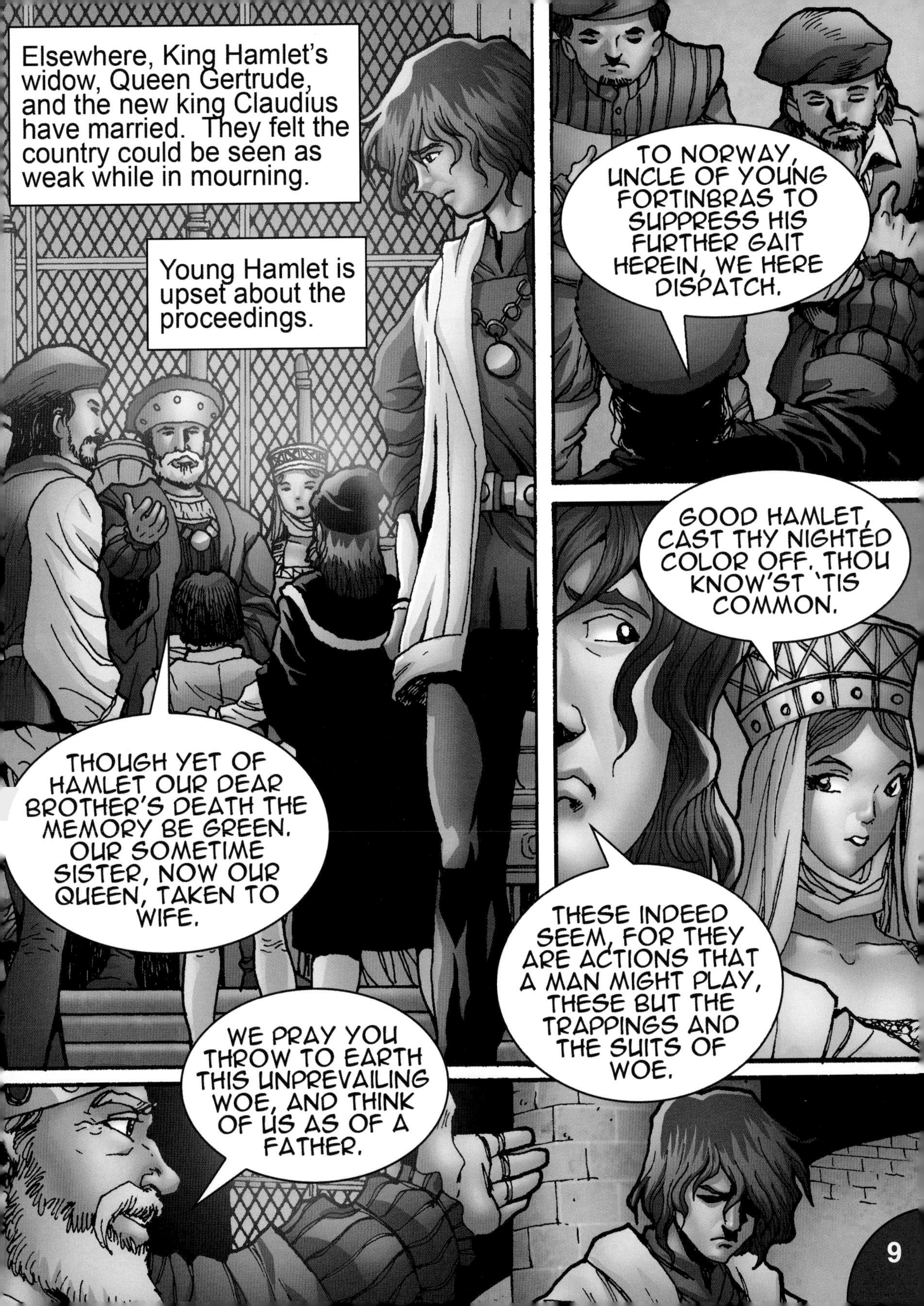

Elsewhere, King Hamlet's widow, Queen Gertrude, and the new king Claudius have married. They felt the country could be seen as weak while in mourning.
Young Hamlet is upset about the proceedings.
THOUGH YET OF HAMLET OUR DEAR BROTHER'S DEATH THE MEMORY BE GREEN. OUR SOMETIME SISTER, NOW OUR QUEEN, TAKEN TO WIFE.
TO NORWAY, UNCLE OF YOUNG FORTINBRAS TO SUPPRESS HIS FURTHER GAIT HEREIN, WE HERE DISPATCH.
GOOD HAMLET, CAST THY NIGHTED COLOR OFF. THOU KNOW'ST 'TIS COMMON.
THESE INDEED SEEM, FOR THEY ARE ACTIONS THAT A MAN MIGHT PLAY, THESE BUT THE TRAPPINGS AND THE SUITS OF WOE.
WE PRAY YOU THROW TO EARTH THIS UNPREVAILING WOE, AND THINK OF US AS OF A FATHER.

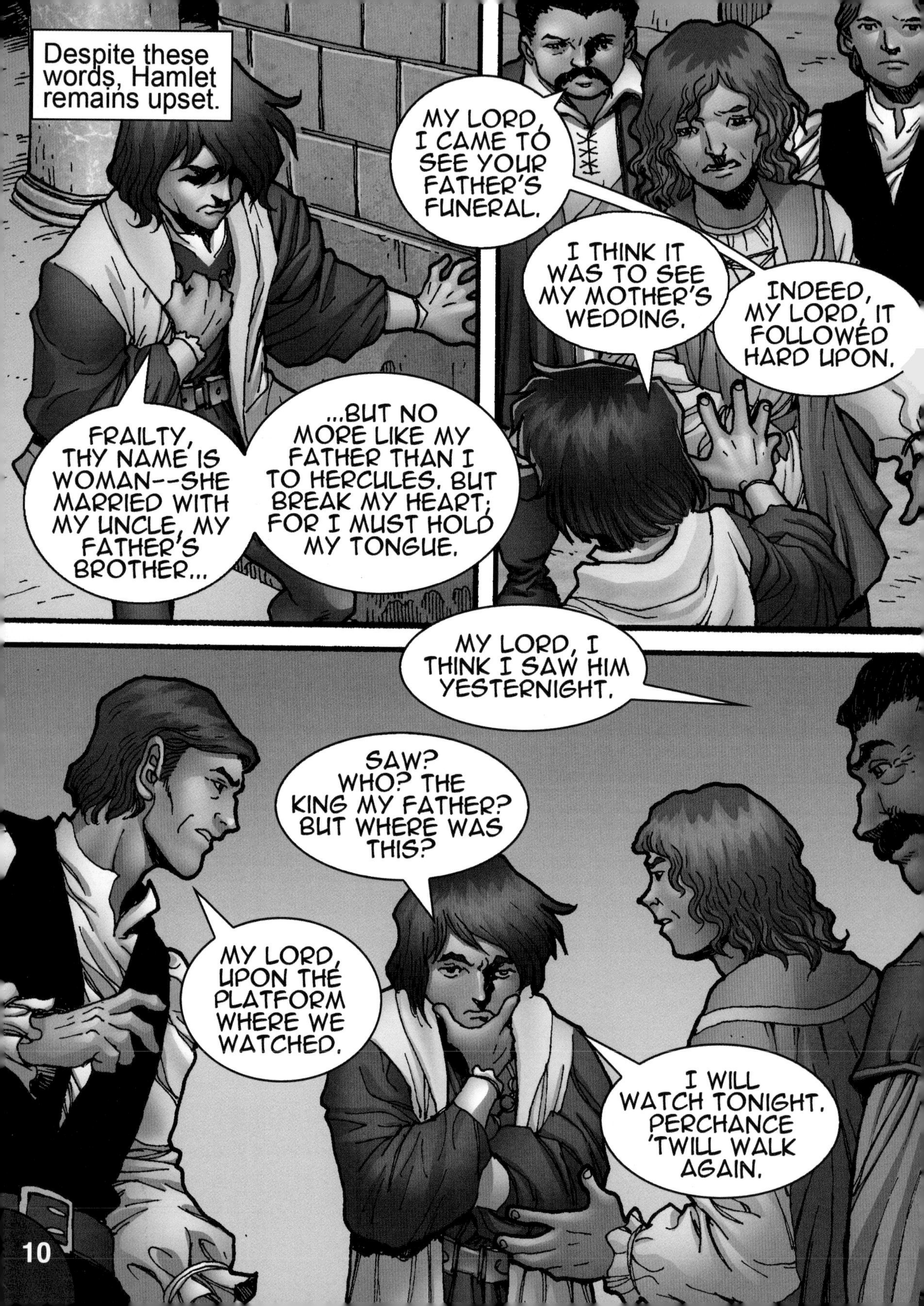
Despite these words, Hamlet remains upset.
FRAILTY, THY NAME IS WOMAN--SHE MARRIED WITH MY UNCLE, MY FATHER'S BROTHER...
...BUT NO MORE LIKE MY FATHER THAN I TO HERCULES. BUT BREAK MY HEART; FOR I MUST HOLD MY TONGUE.
MY LORD, I CAME TO SEE YOUR FATHER'S FUNERAL.
I THINK IT WAS TO SEE MY MOTHER'S WEDDING.
INDEED, MY LORD, IT FOLLOWED HARD UPON.
MY LORD, I THINK I SAW HIM YESTERNIGHT.
SAW? WHO? THE KING MY FATHER? BUT WHERE WAS THIS?
MY LORD, UPON THE PLATFORM WHERE WE WATCHED.
I WILL WATCH TONIGHT. PERCHANCE 'TWILL WALK AGAIN.

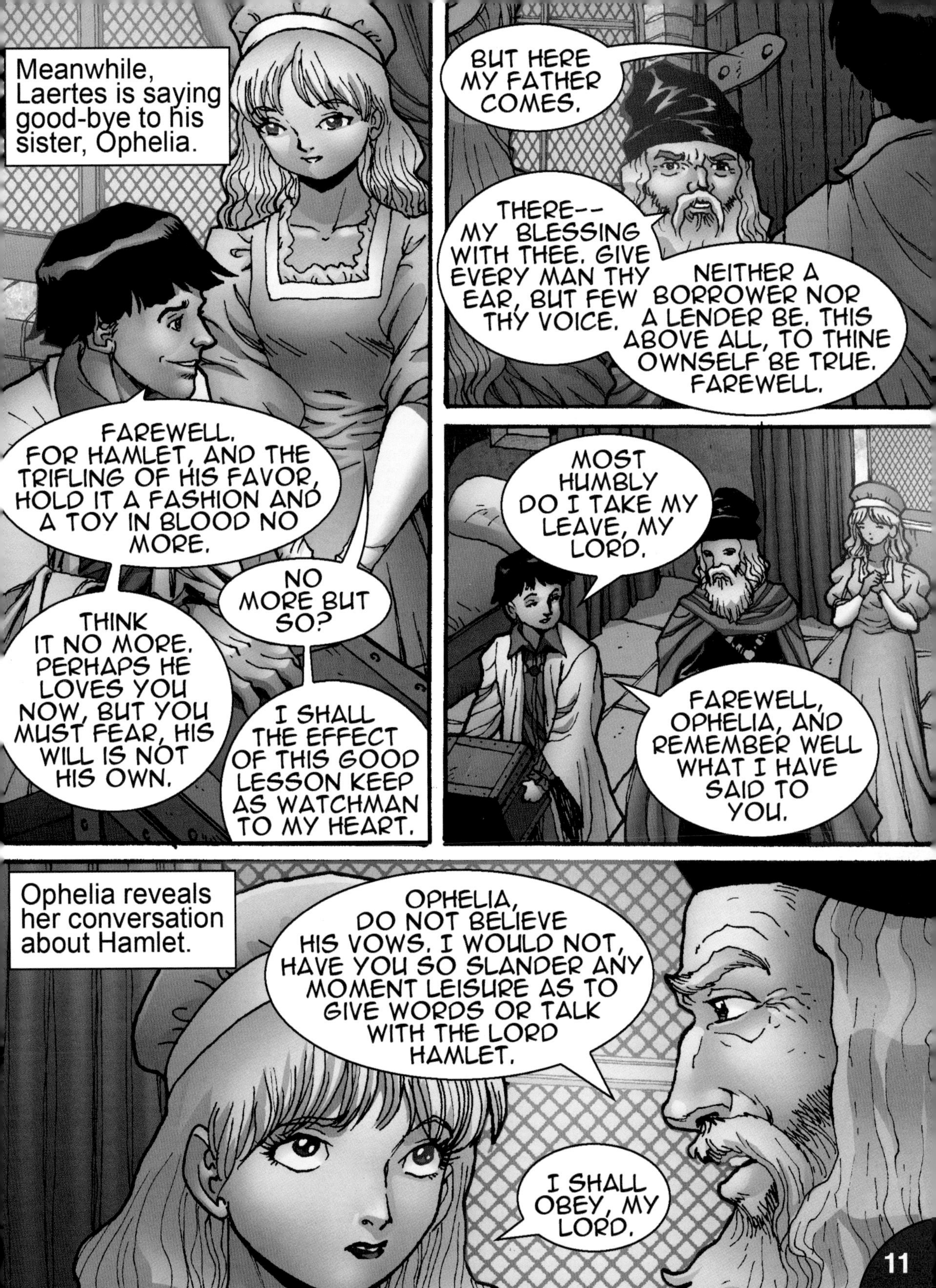

Meanwhile, Laertes is saying good-bye to his sister, Ophelia.
FAREWELL. FOR HAMLET, AND THE TRIFLING OF HIS FAVOR, HOLD IT A FASHION AND A TOY IN BLOOD NO MORE.
NO MORE BUT SO?
THINK IT NO MORE. PERHAPS HE LOVES YOU NOW, BUT YOU MUST FEAR, HIS WILL IS NOT HIS OWN.
I SHALL THE EFFECT OF THIS GOOD LESSON KEEP AS WATCHMAN TO MY HEART.
BUT HERE MY FATHER COMES.
THERE-- MY BLESSING WITH THEE. GIVE EVERY MAN THY EAR, BUT FEW THY VOICE.
NEITHER A BORROWER NOR A LENDER BE. THIS ABOVE ALL, TO THINE OWNSELF BE TRUE. FAREWELL.
MOST HUMBLY DO I TAKE MY LEAVE, MY LORD.
FAREWELL, OPHELIA, AND REMEMBER WELL WHAT I HAVE SAID TO YOU.
Ophelia reveals her conversation about Hamlet.
OPHELIA, DO NOT BELIEVE HIS VOWS. I WOULD NOT, HAVE YOU SO SLANDER ANY MOMENT LEISURE AS TO GIVE WORDS OR TALK WITH THE LORD HAMLET.
I SHALL OBEY, MY LORD.

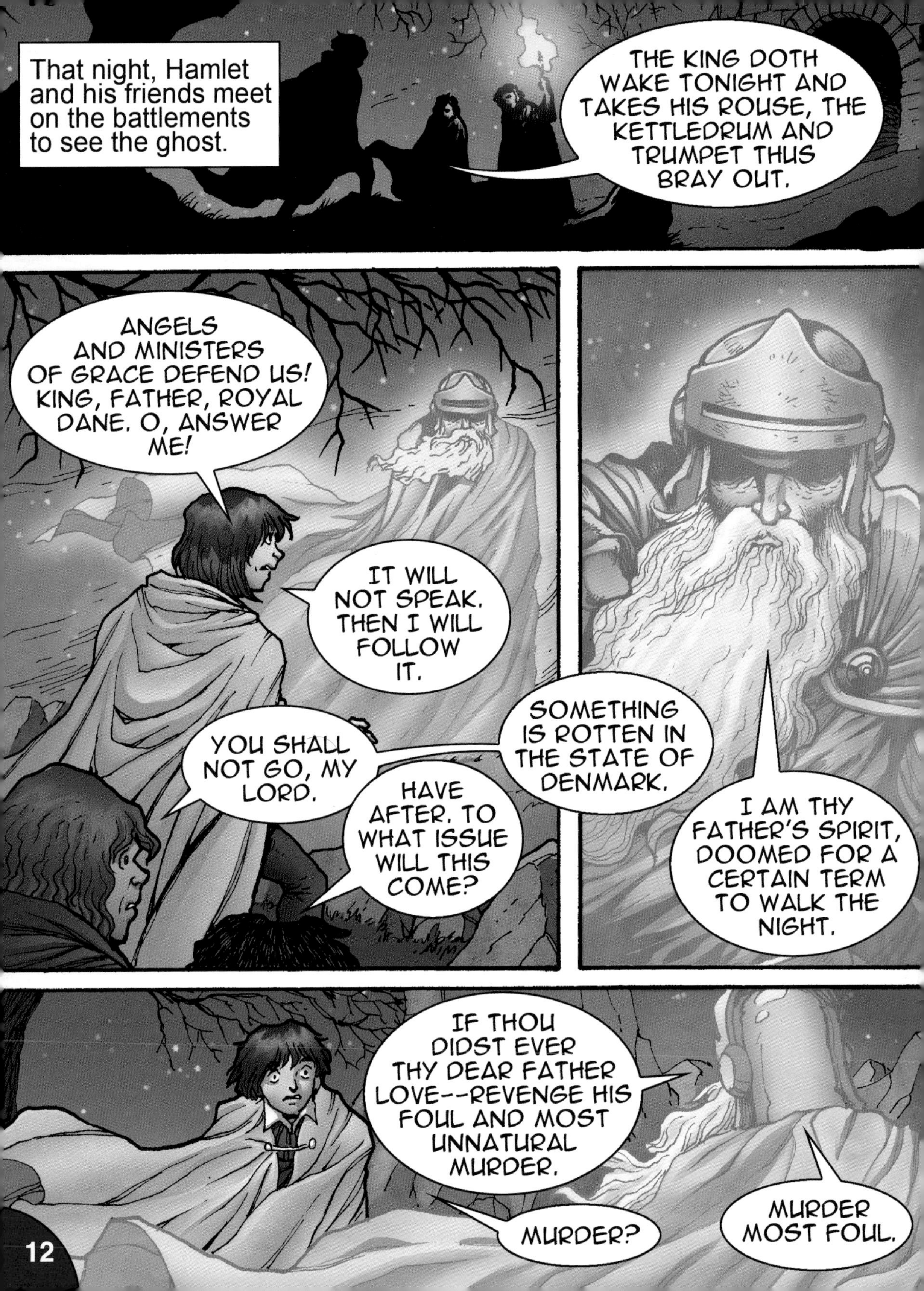
That night, Hamlet and his friends meet on the battlements to see the ghost.
THE KING DOTH WAKE TONIGHT AND TAKES HIS ROUSE, THE KETTLEDRUM AND TRUMPET THUS BRAY OUT.
ANGELS AND MINISTERS OF GRACE DEFEND US! KING, FATHER, ROYAL DANE. O, ANSWER ME!
IT WILL NOT SPEAK. THEN I WILL FOLLOW IT.
YOU SHALL NOT GO, MY LORD.
HAVE AFTER. TO WHAT ISSUE WILL THIS COME?
SOMETHING IS ROTTEN IN THE STATE OF DENMARK.
I AM THY FATHER'S SPIRIT, DOOMED FOR A CERTAIN TERM TO WALK THE NIGHT.
IF THOU DIDST EVER THY DEAR FATHER LOVE--REVENGE HIS FOUL AND MOST UNNATURAL MURDER.
MURDER?
MURDER MOST FOUL.

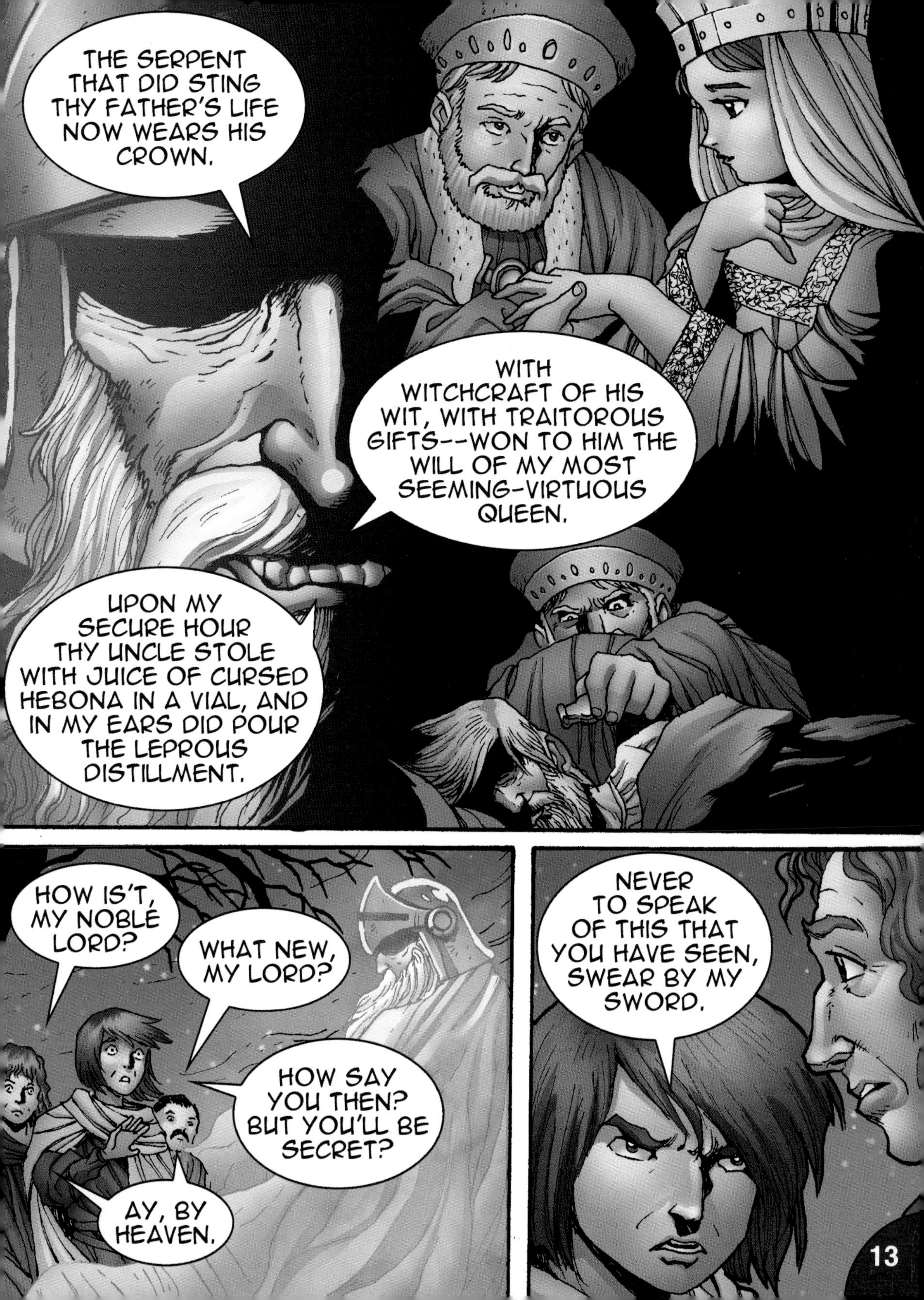
THE SERPENT THAT DID STING THY FATHER'S LIFE NOW WEARS HIS CROWN.
WITH WITCHCRAFT OF HIS WIT, WITH TRAITOROUS GIFTS--WON TO HIM THE WILL OF MY MOST SEEMING-VIRTUOUS QUEEN.
UPON MY SECURE HOUR THY UNCLE STOLE WITH JUICE OF CURSED HEBONA IN A VIAL, AND IN MY EARS DID POUR THE LEPROUS DISTILLMENT.
HOW IS'T, MY NOBLE LORD?
WHAT NEW, MY LORD?
HOW SAY YOU THEN? BUT YOU'LL BE SECRET?
AY, BY HEAVEN.
NEVER TO SPEAK OF THIS THAT YOU HAVE SEEN, SWEAR BY MY SWORD.

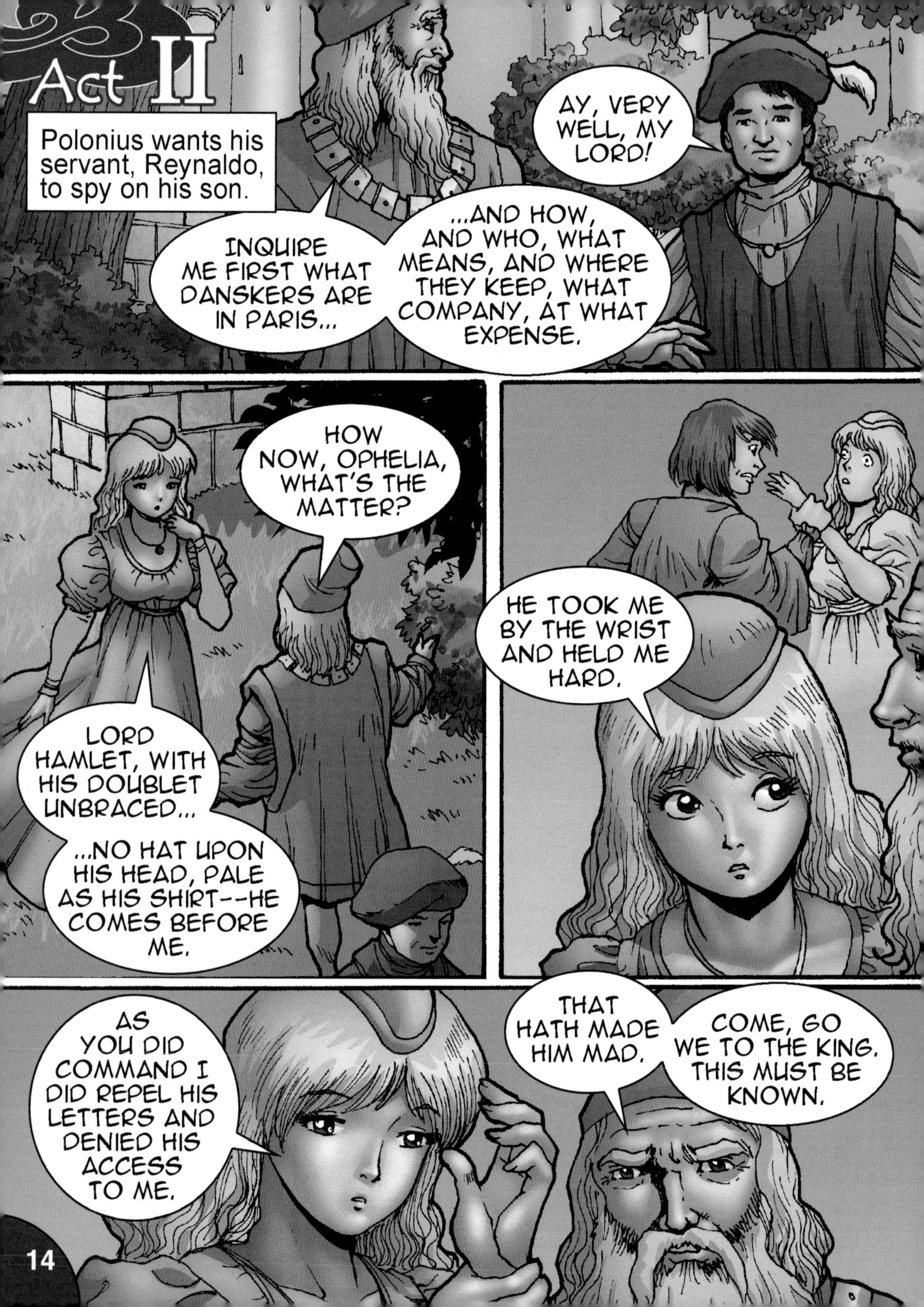
Act II
Polonius wants his servant, Reynaldo, to spy on his son.
INQUIRE ME FIRST WHAT DANSKERS ARE IN PARIS...
...AND HOW, AND WHO, WHAT MEANS, AND WHERE THEY KEEP, WHAT COMPANY, AT WHAT EXPENSE.
AY, VERY WELL, MY LORD!
HOW NOW, OPHELIA, WHAT'S THE MATTER?
LORD HAMLET, WITH HIS DOUBLET UNBRACED...
...NO HAT UPON HIS HEAD, PALE AS HIS SHIRT--HE COMES BEFORE ME.
HE TOOK ME BY THE WRIST AND HELD ME HARD.
AS YOU DID COMMAND I DID REPEL HIS LETTERS AND DENIED HIS ACCESS TO ME.
THAT HATH MADE HIM MAD.
COME, GO WE TO THE KING. THIS MUST BE KNOWN.

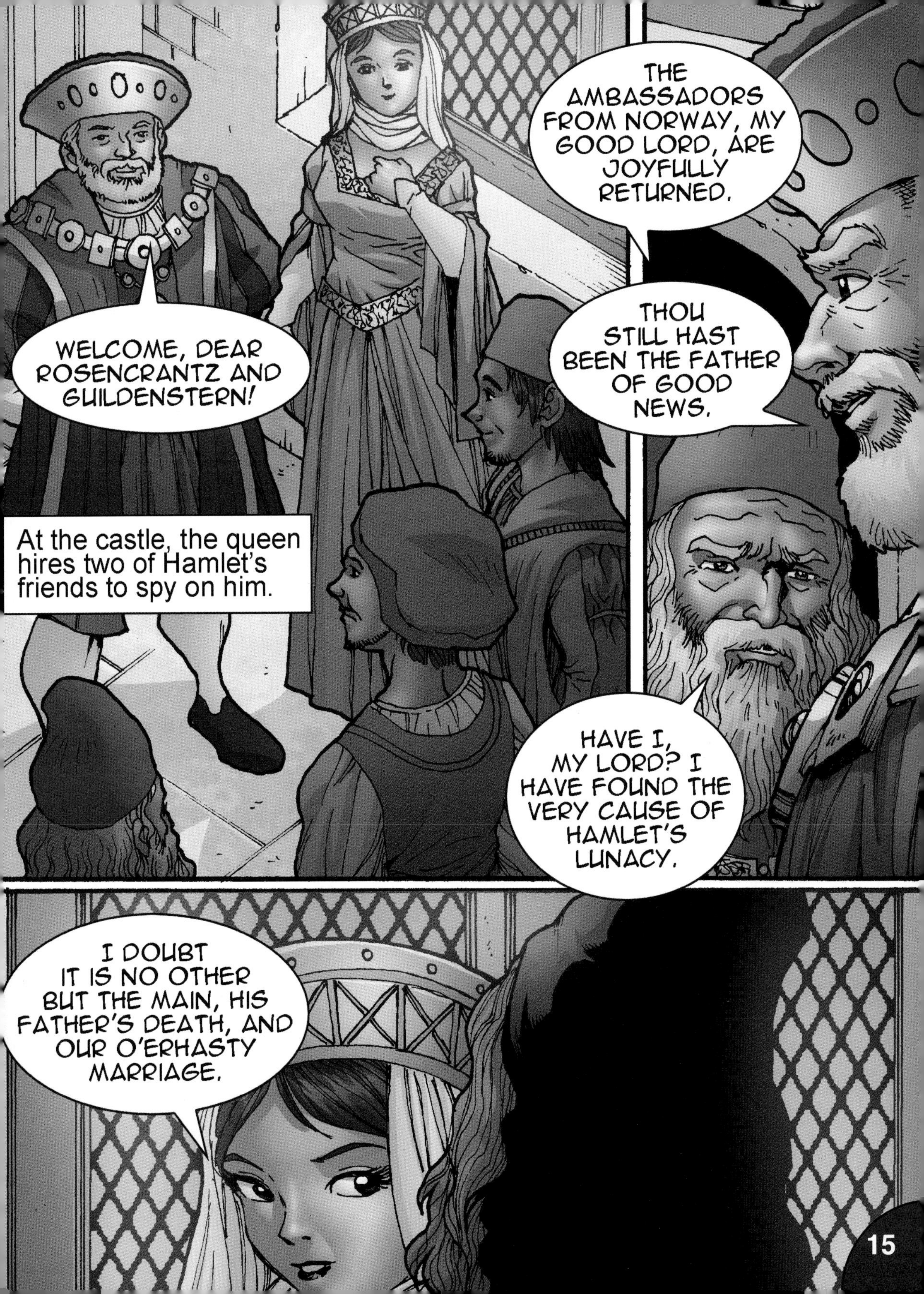
WELCOME, DEAR ROSENCRANTZ AND GUILDENSTERN!
At the castle, the queen hires two of Hamlet's friends to spy on him.
THE AMBASSADORS FROM NORWAY, MY GOOD LORD, ARE JOYFULLY RETURNED.
THOU STILL HAST BEEN THE FATHER OF GOOD NEWS.
HAVE I, MY LORD? I HAVE FOUND THE VERY CAUSE OF HAMLET'S LUNACY.
I DOUBT IT IS NO OTHER BUT THE MAIN, HIS FATHER'S DEATH, AND OUR O'ERHASTY MARRIAGE.

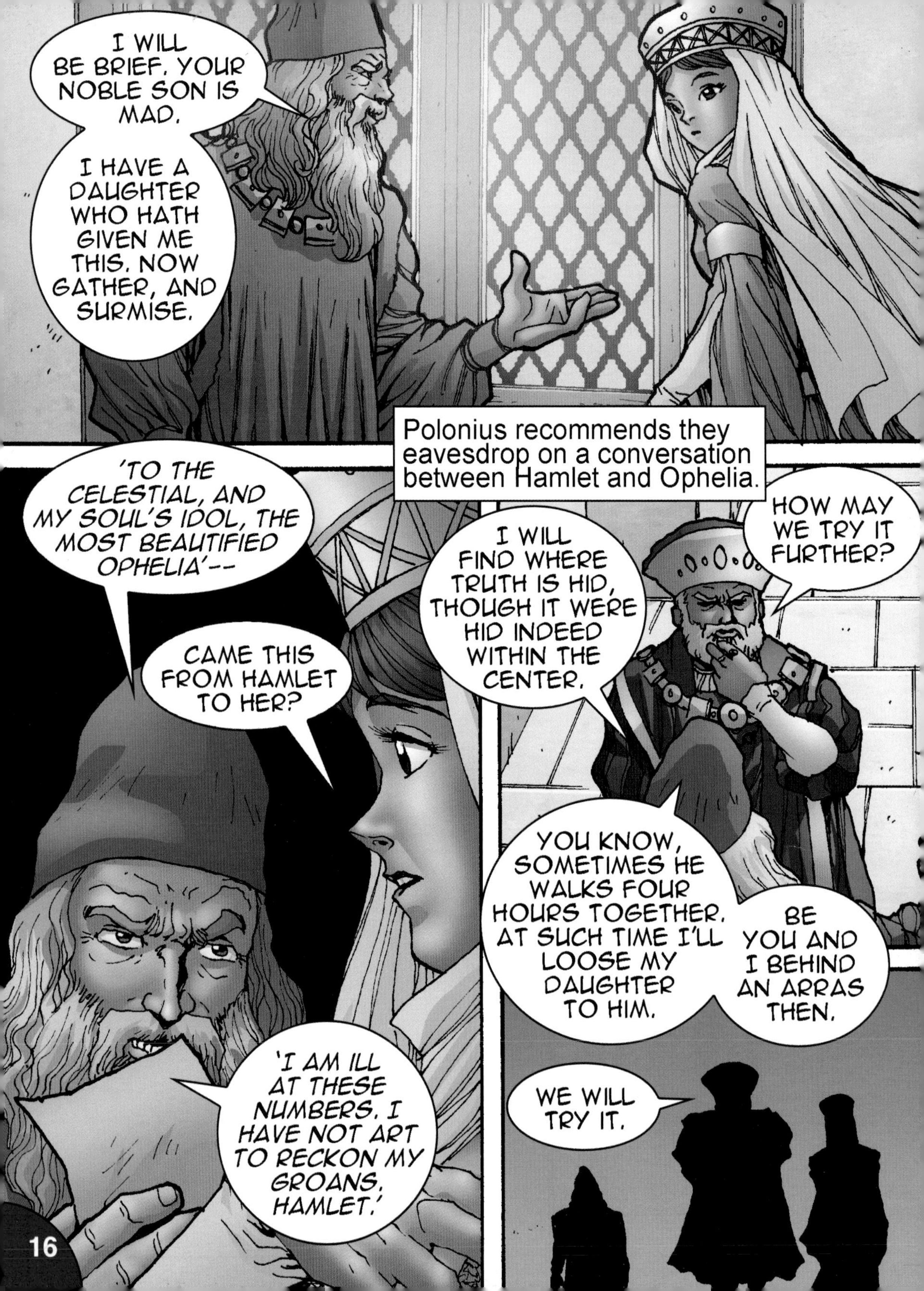
I WILL BE BRIEF. YOUR NOBLE SON IS MAD.
I HAVE A DAUGHTER WHO HATH GIVEN ME THIS. NOW GATHER, AND SURMISE.
Polonius recommends they eavesdrop on a conversation between Hamlet and Ophelia.
'TO THE CELESTIAL, AND MY SOUL'S IDOL, THE MOST BEAUTIFIED OPHELIA'--
CAME THIS FROM HAMLET TO HER?
'I AM ILL AT THESE NUMBERS. I HAVE NOT ART TO RECKON MY GROANS, HAMLET.'
HOW MAY WE TRY IT FURTHER?
I WILL FIND WHERE TRUTH IS HID, THOUGH IT WERE HID INDEED WITHIN THE CENTER.
YOU KNOW, SOMETIMES HE WALKS FOUR HOURS TOGETHER. AT SUCH TIME I'LL LOOSE MY DAUGHTER TO HIM.
BE YOU AND I BEHIND AN ARRAS THEN.
WE WILL TRY IT.

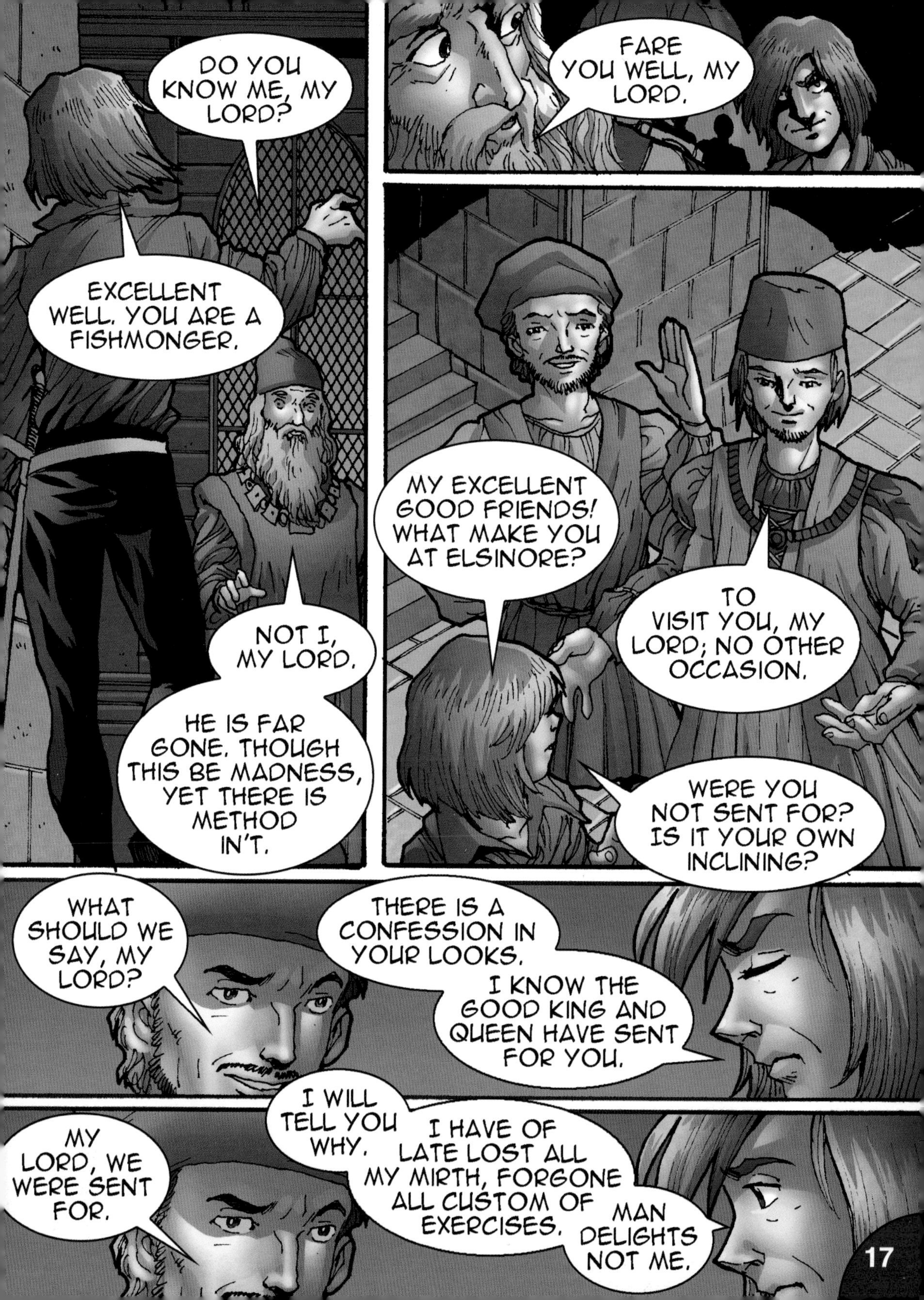
DO YOU KNOW ME, MY LORD?
EXCELLENT WELL. YOU ARE A FISHMONGER.
NOT I, MY LORD.
HE IS FAR GONE. THOUGH THIS BE MADNESS, YET THERE IS METHOD IN'T.
FARE YOU WELL, MY LORD.
MY EXCELLENT GOOD FRIENDS! WHAT MAKE YOU AT ELSINORE?
TO VISIT YOU, MY LORD; NO OTHER OCCASION.
WERE YOU NOT SENT FOR? IS IT YOUR OWN INCLINING?
WHAT SHOULD WE SAY, MY LORD?
THERE IS A CONFESSION IN YOUR LOOKS.
I KNOW THE GOOD KING AND QUEEN HAVE SENT FOR YOU.
MY LORD, WE WERE SENT FOR.
I WILL TELL YOU WHY.
I HAVE OF LATE LOST ALL MY MIRTH, FORGONE ALL CUSTOM OF EXERCISES.
MAN DELIGHTS NOT ME.

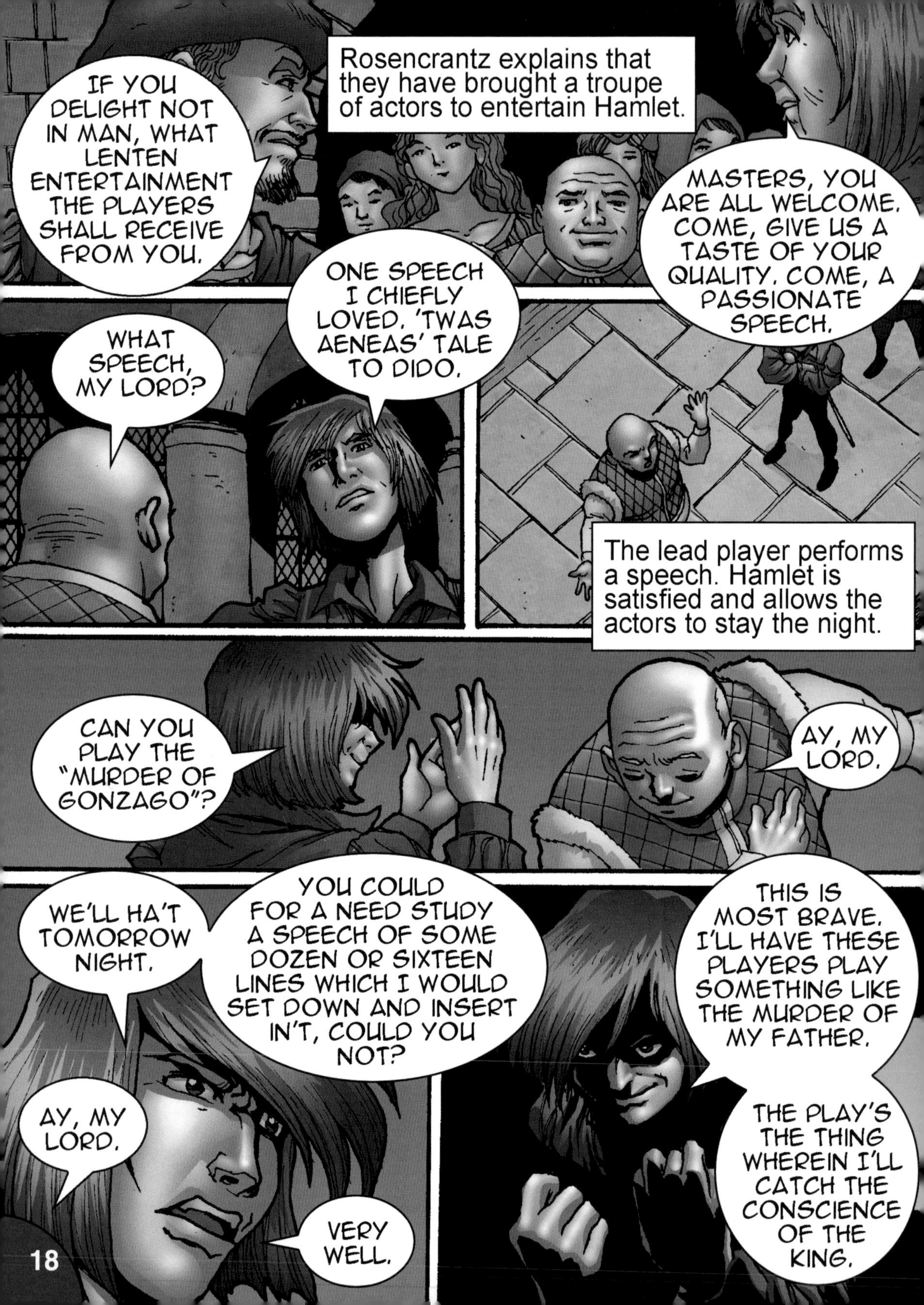
Rosencrantz explains that they have brought a troupe of actors to entertain Hamlet.
IF YOU DELIGHT NOT IN MAN, WHAT LENTEN ENTERTAINMENT THE PLAYERS SHALL RECEIVE FROM YOU.
MASTERS, YOU ARE ALL WELCOME. COME, GIVE US A TASTE OF YOUR QUALITY. COME, A PASSIONATE SPEECH.
WHAT SPEECH, MY LORD?
ONE SPEECH I CHIEFLY LOVED. 'TWAS AENEAS' TALE TO DIDO.
The lead player performs a speech. Hamlet is satisfied and allows the actors to stay the night.
CAN YOU PLAY THE "MURDER OF GONZAGO"?
AY, MY LORD.
WE'LL HA'T TOMORROW NIGHT.
YOU COULD FOR A NEED STUDY A SPEECH OF SOME DOZEN OR SIXTEEN LINES WHICH I WOULD SET DOWN AND INSERT IN'T, COULD YOU NOT?
AY, MY LORD.
VERY WELL.
THIS IS MOST BRAVE. I'LL HAVE THESE PLAYERS PLAY SOMETHING LIKE THE MURDER OF MY FATHER.
THE PLAY'S THE THING WHEREIN I'LL CATCH THE CONSCIENCE OF THE KING.

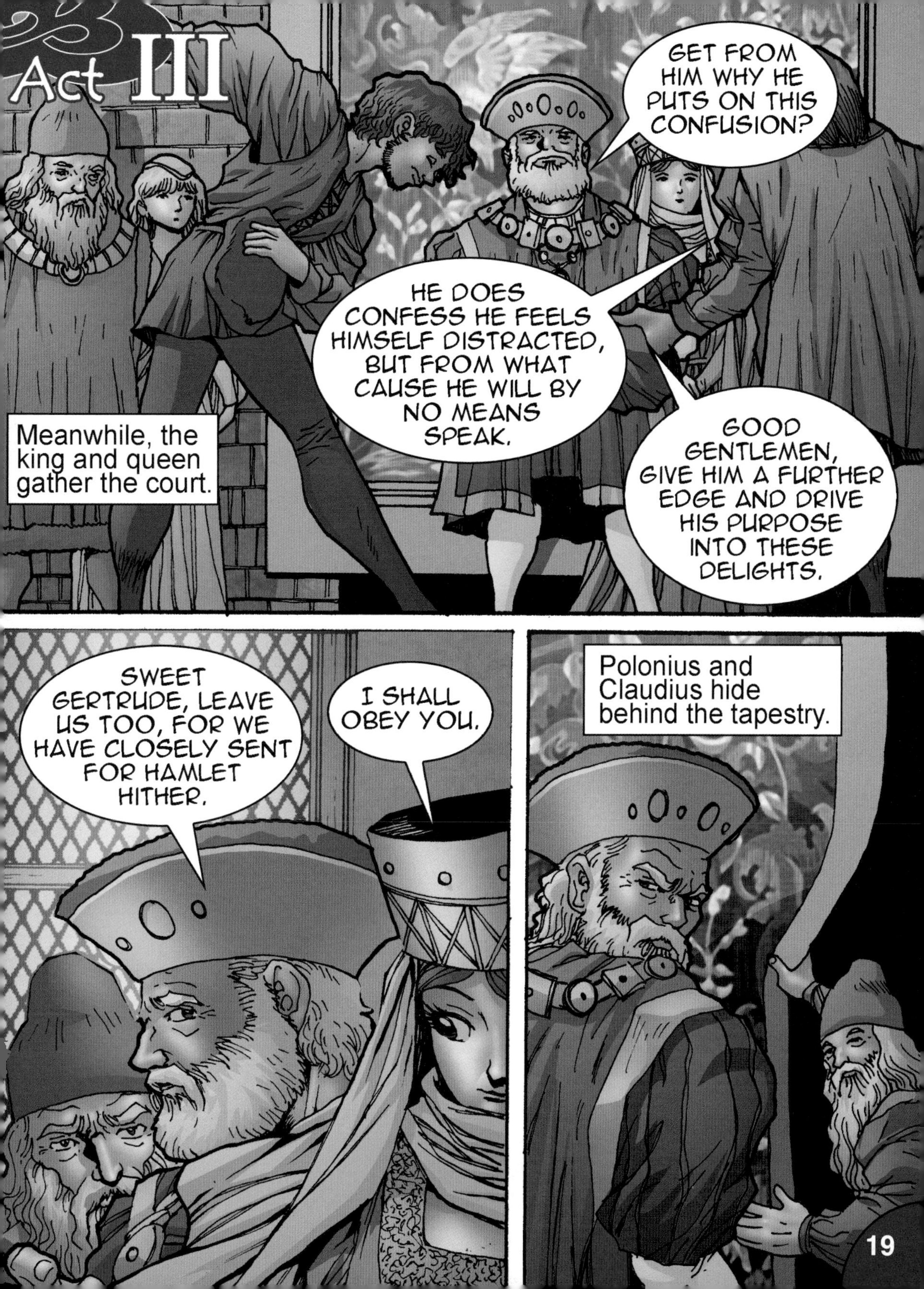
Act III
GET FROM HIM WHY HE PUTS ON THIS CONFUSION?
HE DOES CONFESS HE FEELS HIMSELF DISTRACTED, BUT FROM WHAT CAUSE HE WILL BY NO MEANS SPEAK.
Meanwhile, the king and queen gather the court.
GOOD GENTLEMEN, GIVE HIM A FURTHER EDGE AND DRIVE HIS PURPOSE INTO THESE DELIGHTS.
SWEET GERTRUDE, LEAVE US TOO, FOR WE HAVE CLOSELY SENT FOR HAMLET HITHER.
I SHALL OBEY YOU.
Polonius and Claudius hide behind the tapestry.

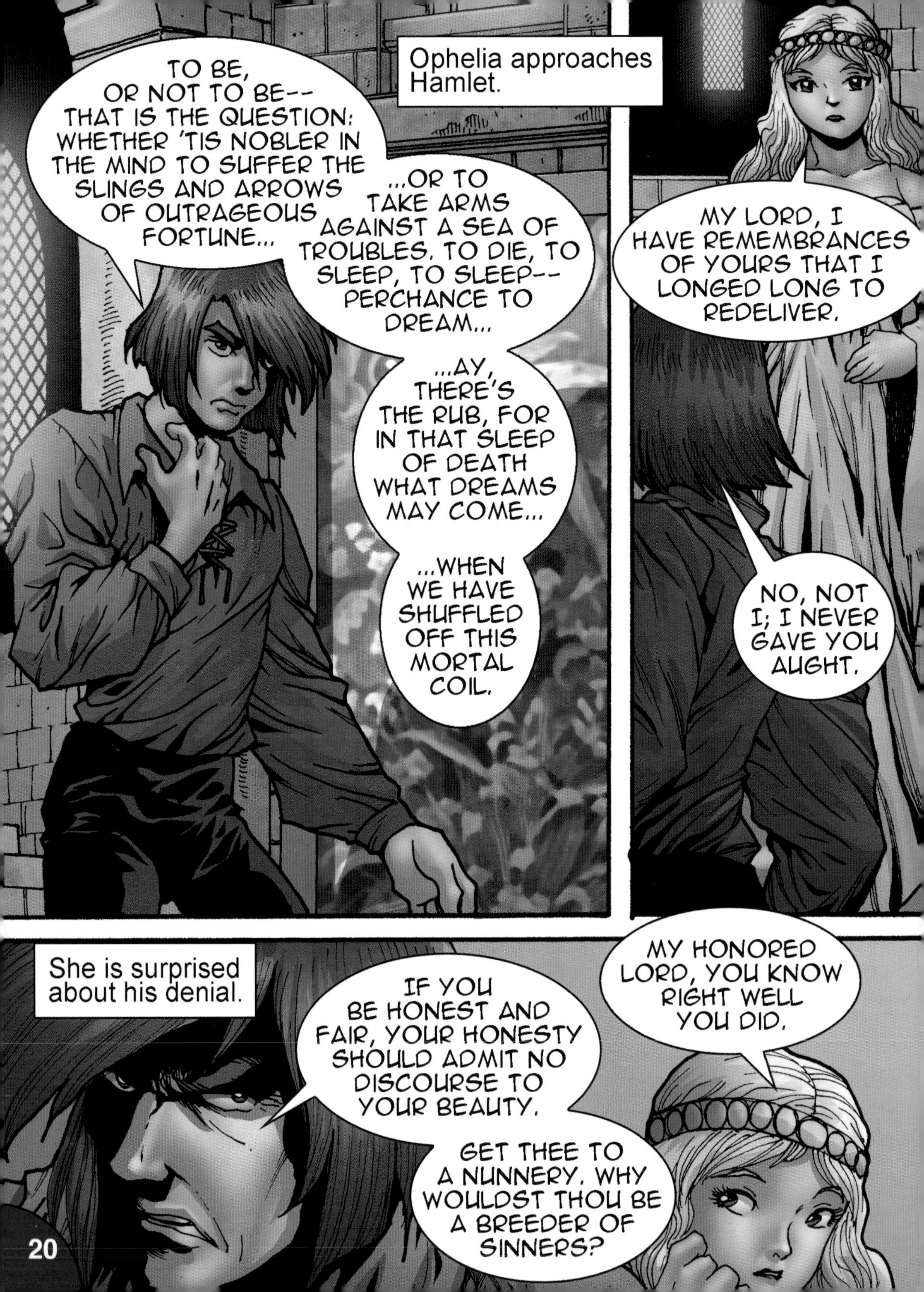
Ophelia approaches Hamlet.
TO BE, OR NOT TO BE-- THAT IS THE QUESTION: WHETHER 'TIS NOBLER IN THE MIND TO SUFFER THE SLINGS AND ARROWS OF OUTRAGEOUS FORTUNE...
...OR TO TAKE ARMS AGAINST A SEA OF TROUBLES. TO DIE, TO SLEEP, TO SLEEP-- PERCHANCE TO DREAM...
...AY, THERE'S THE RUB, FOR IN THAT SLEEP OF DEATH WHAT DREAMS MAY COME...
...WHEN WE HAVE SHUFFLED OFF THIS MORTAL COIL.
MY LORD, I HAVE REMEMBRANCES OF YOURS THAT I LONGED LONG TO REDELIVER.
NO, NOT I; I NEVER GAVE YOU AUGHT.
She is surprised about his denial.
MY HONORED LORD, YOU KNOW RIGHT WELL YOU DID.
IF YOU BE HONEST AND FAIR, YOUR HONESTY SHOULD ADMIT NO DISCOURSE TO YOUR BEAUTY.
GET THEE TO A NUNNERY. WHY WOULDST THOU BE A BREEDER OF SINNERS?

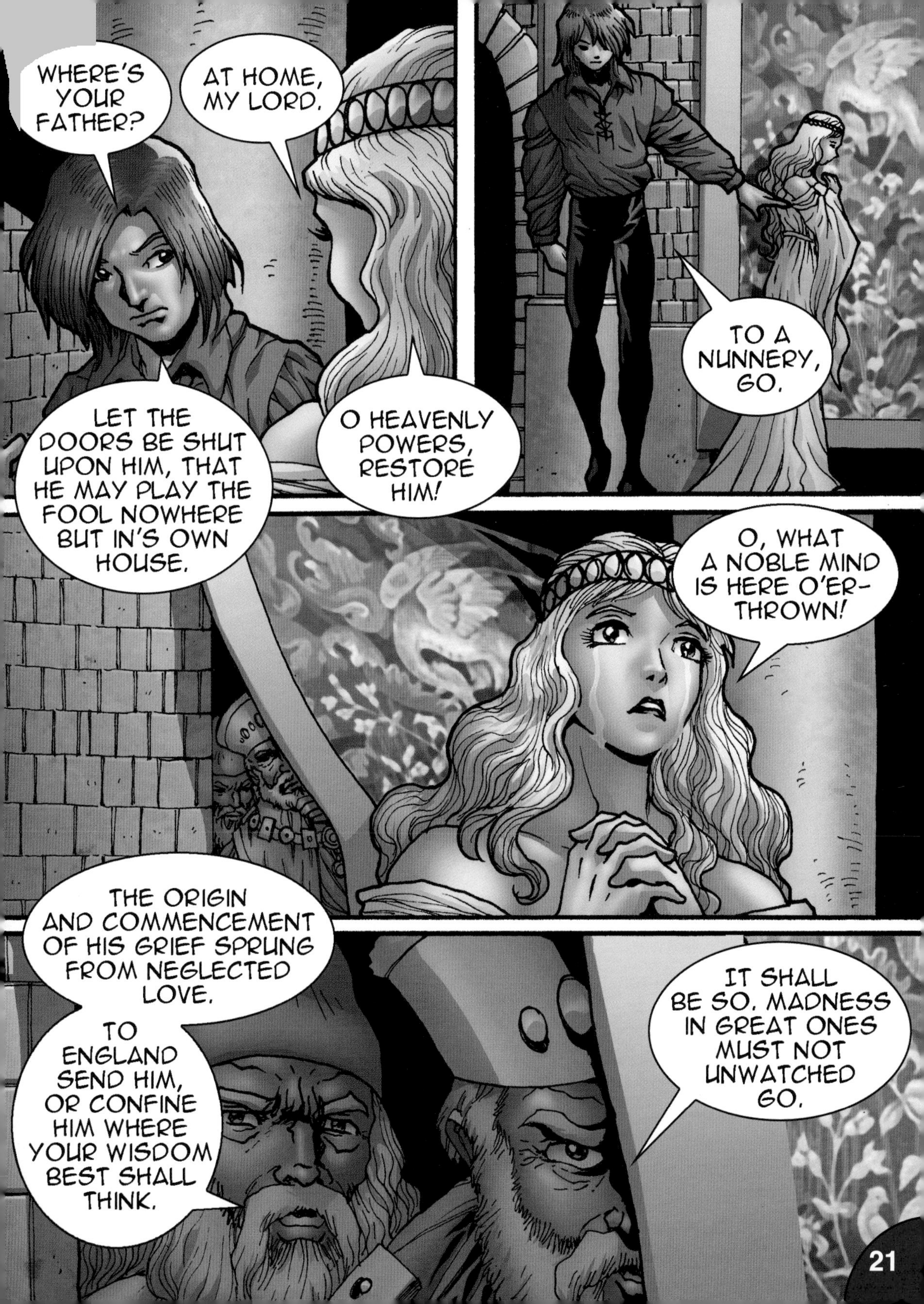
WHERE'S YOUR FATHER?
AT HOME, MY LORD.
LET THE DOORS BE SHUT UPON HIM, THAT HE MAY PLAY THE FOOL NOWHERE BUT IN'S OWN HOUSE.
O HEAVENLY POWERS, RESTORE HIM!
TO A NUNNERY, GO.
O, WHAT A NOBLE MIND IS HERE O'ER-THROWN!
THE ORIGIN AND COMMENCEMENT OF HIS GRIEF SPRUNG FROM NEGLECTED LOVE.
TO ENGLAND SEND HIM, OR CONFINE HIM WHERE YOUR WISDOM BEST SHALL THINK.
IT SHALL BE SO. MADNESS IN GREAT ONES MUST NOT UNWATCHED GO.

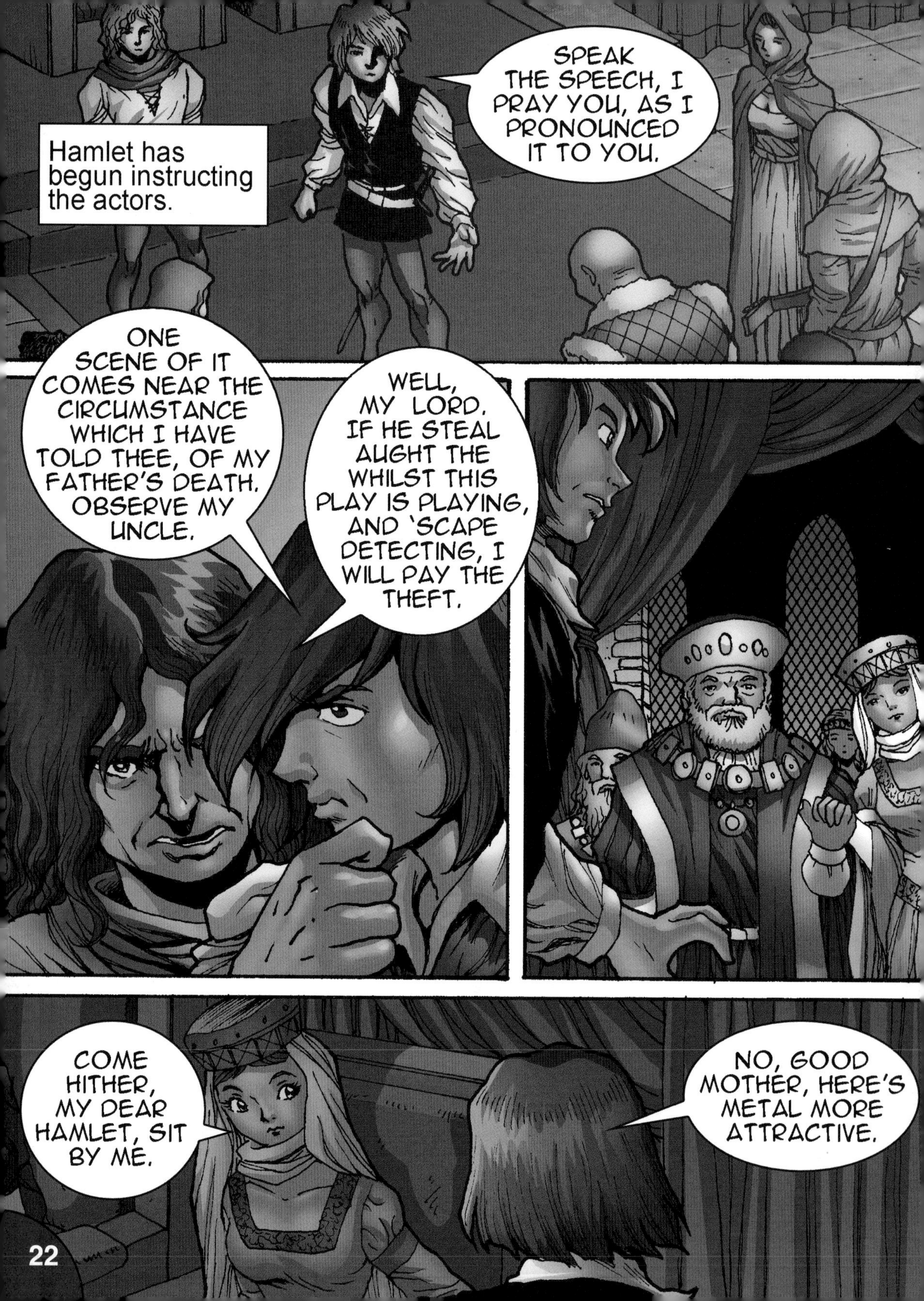
Hamlet has begun instructing the actors.
SPEAK THE SPEECH, I PRAY YOU, AS I PRONOUNCED IT TO YOU.
ONE SCENE OF IT COMES NEAR THE CIRCUMSTANCE WHICH I HAVE TOLD THEE, OF MY FATHER'S DEATH. OBSERVE MY UNCLE.
WELL, MY LORD. IF HE STEAL AUGHT THE WHILST THIS PLAY IS PLAYING, AND 'SCAPE DETECTING, I WILL PAY THE THEFT.
COME HITHER, MY DEAR HAMLET, SIT BY ME.
NO, GOOD MOTHER, HERE'S METAL MORE ATTRACTIVE.

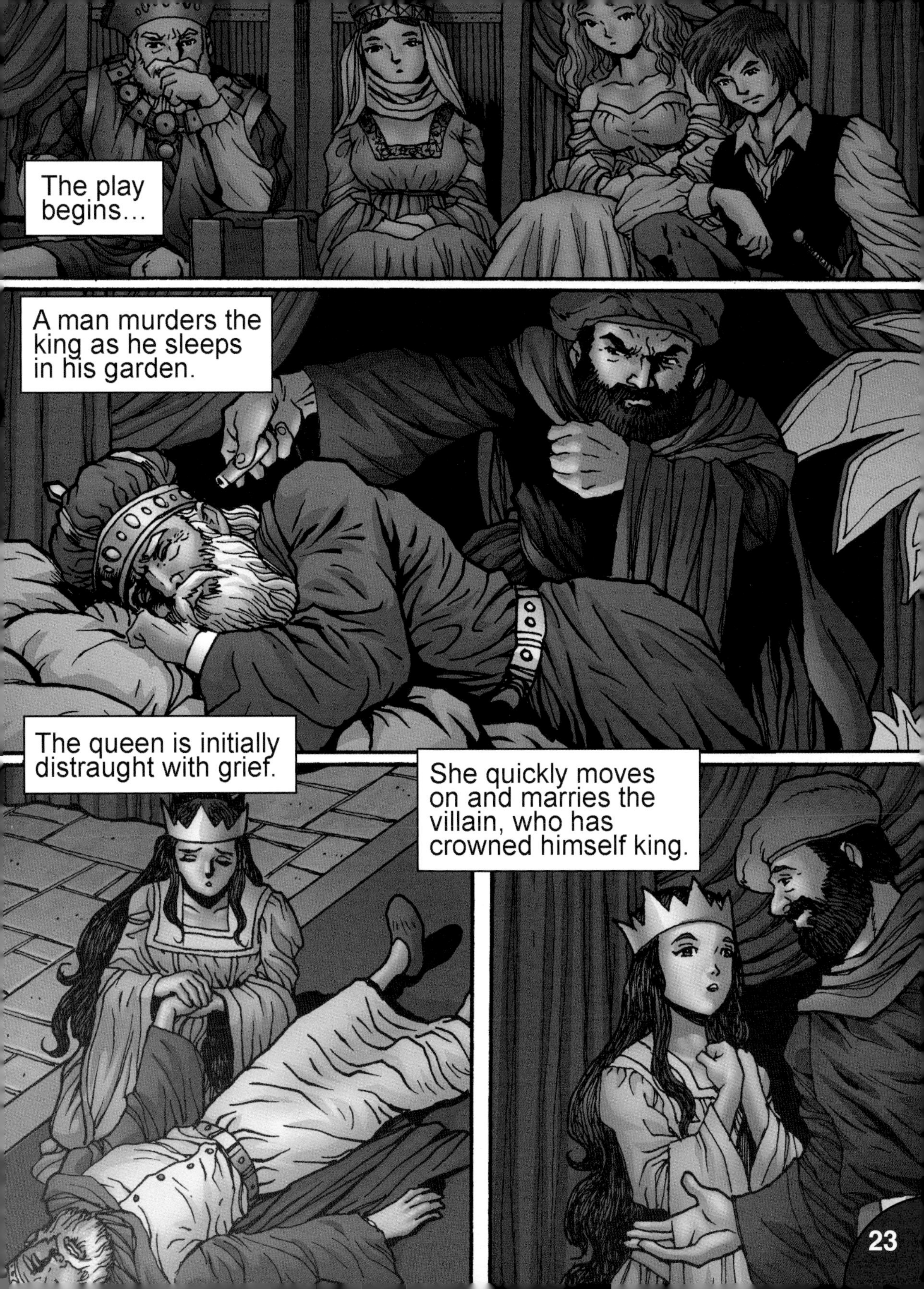

The play begins…
A man murders the king as he sleeps in his garden.
The queen is initially distraught with grief.
She quickly moves on and marries the villain, who has crowned himself king.

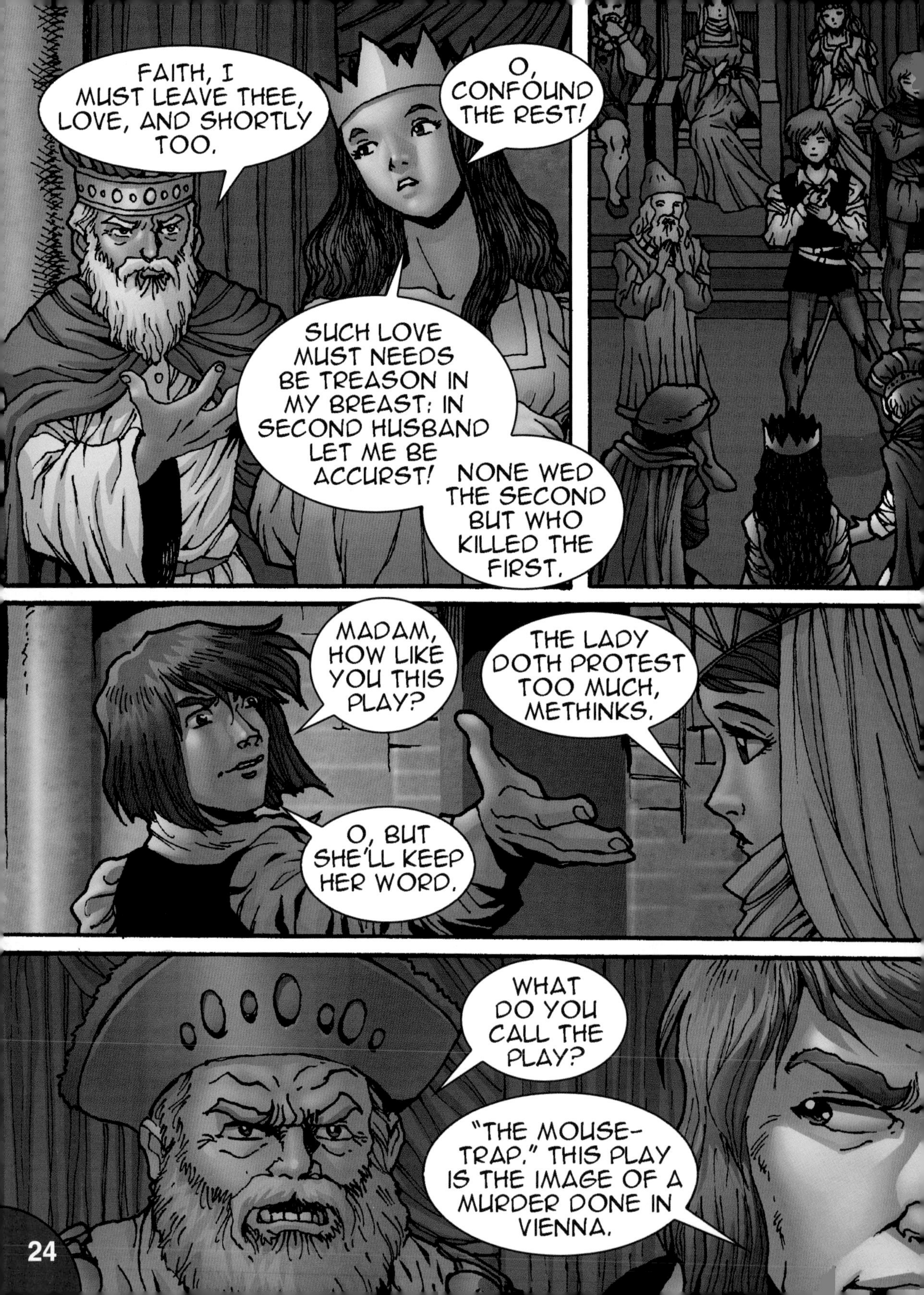
FAITH, I MUST LEAVE THEE, LOVE, AND SHORTLY TOO.
O, CONFOUND THE REST!
SUCH LOVE MUST NEEDS BE TREASON IN MY BREAST: IN SECOND HUSBAND LET ME BE ACCURST!
NONE WED THE SECOND BUT WHO KILLED THE FIRST.
MADAM, HOW LIKE YOU THIS PLAY?
THE LADY DOTH PROTEST TOO MUCH, METHINKS.
O, BUT SHE'LL KEEP HER WORD.
WHAT DO YOU CALL THE PLAY?
"THE MOUSE-TRAP." THIS PLAY IS THE IMAGE OF A MURDER DONE IN VIENNA.

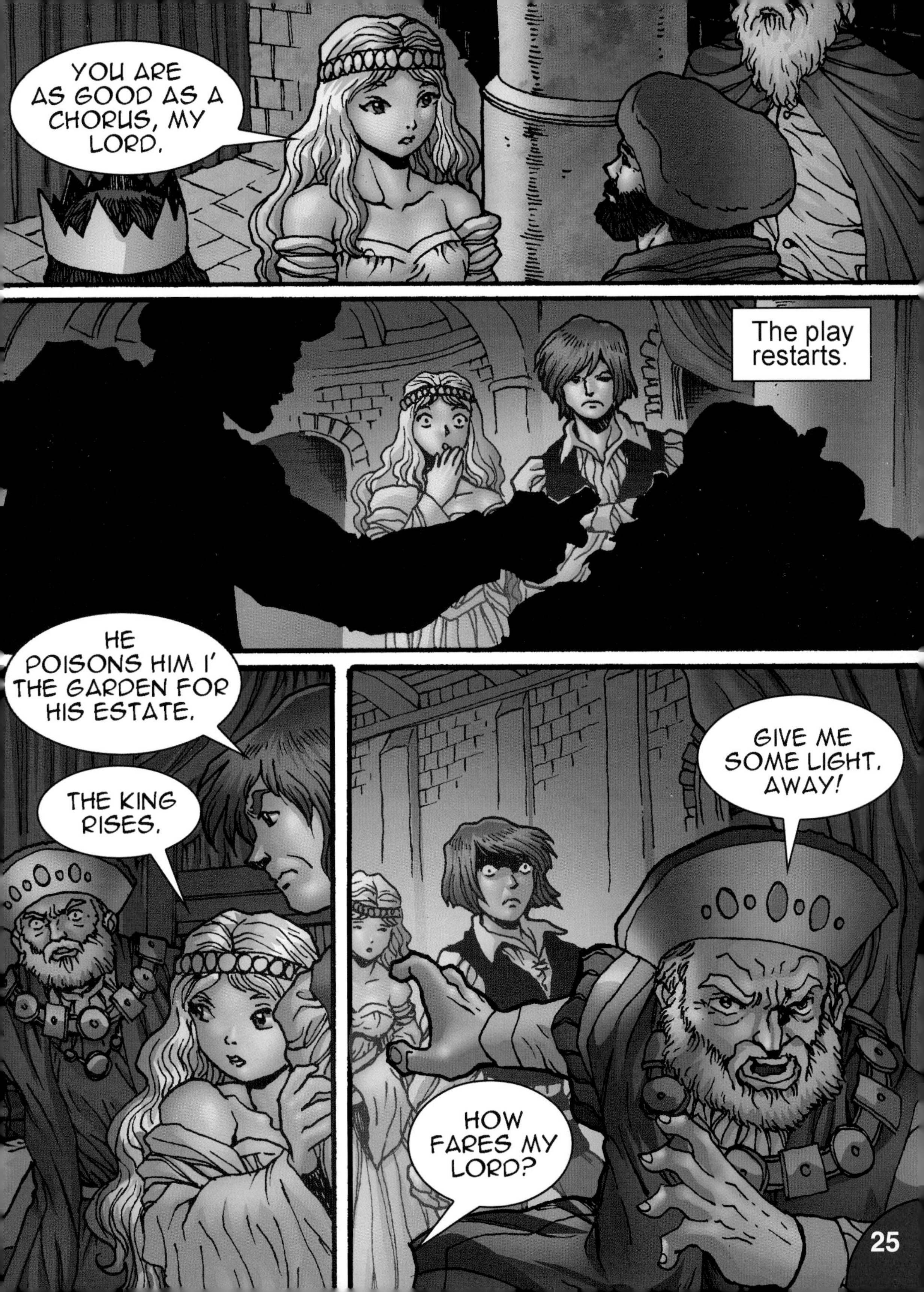
YOU ARE AS GOOD AS A CHORUS, MY LORD.
The play restarts.
HE POISONS HIM I' THE GARDEN FOR HIS ESTATE.
THE KING RISES.
GIVE ME SOME LIGHT. AWAY!
HOW FARES MY LORD?

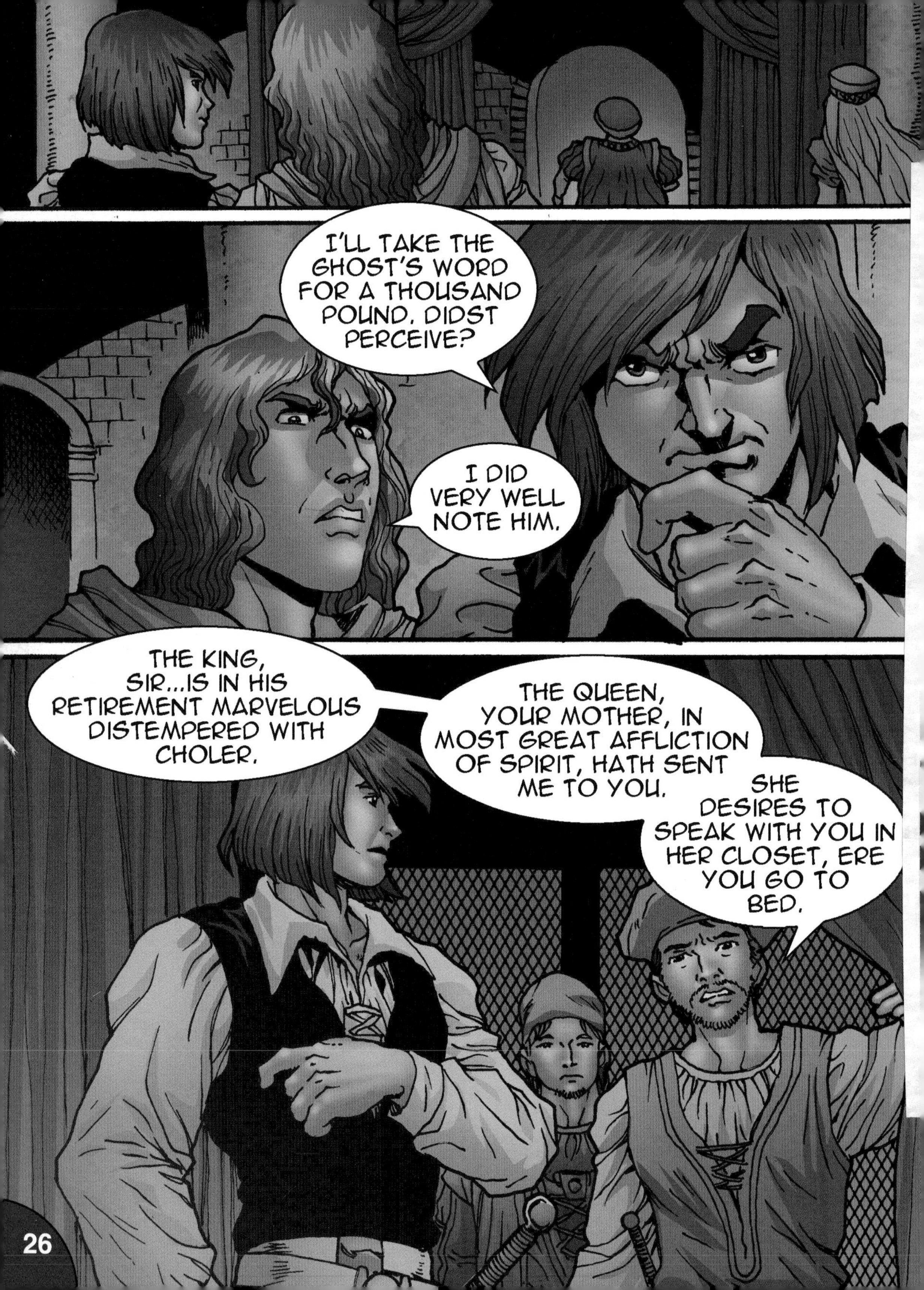
I'LL TAKE THE GHOST'S WORD FOR A THOUSAND POUND. DIDST PERCEIVE?
I DID VERY WELL NOTE HIM.
THE KING, SIR...IS IN HIS RETIREMENT MARVELOUS DISTEMPERED WITH CHOLER.
THE QUEEN, YOUR MOTHER, IN MOST GREAT AFFLICTION OF SPIRIT, HATH SENT ME TO YOU.
SHE DESIRES TO SPEAK WITH YOU IN HER CLOSET, ERE YOU GO TO BED.

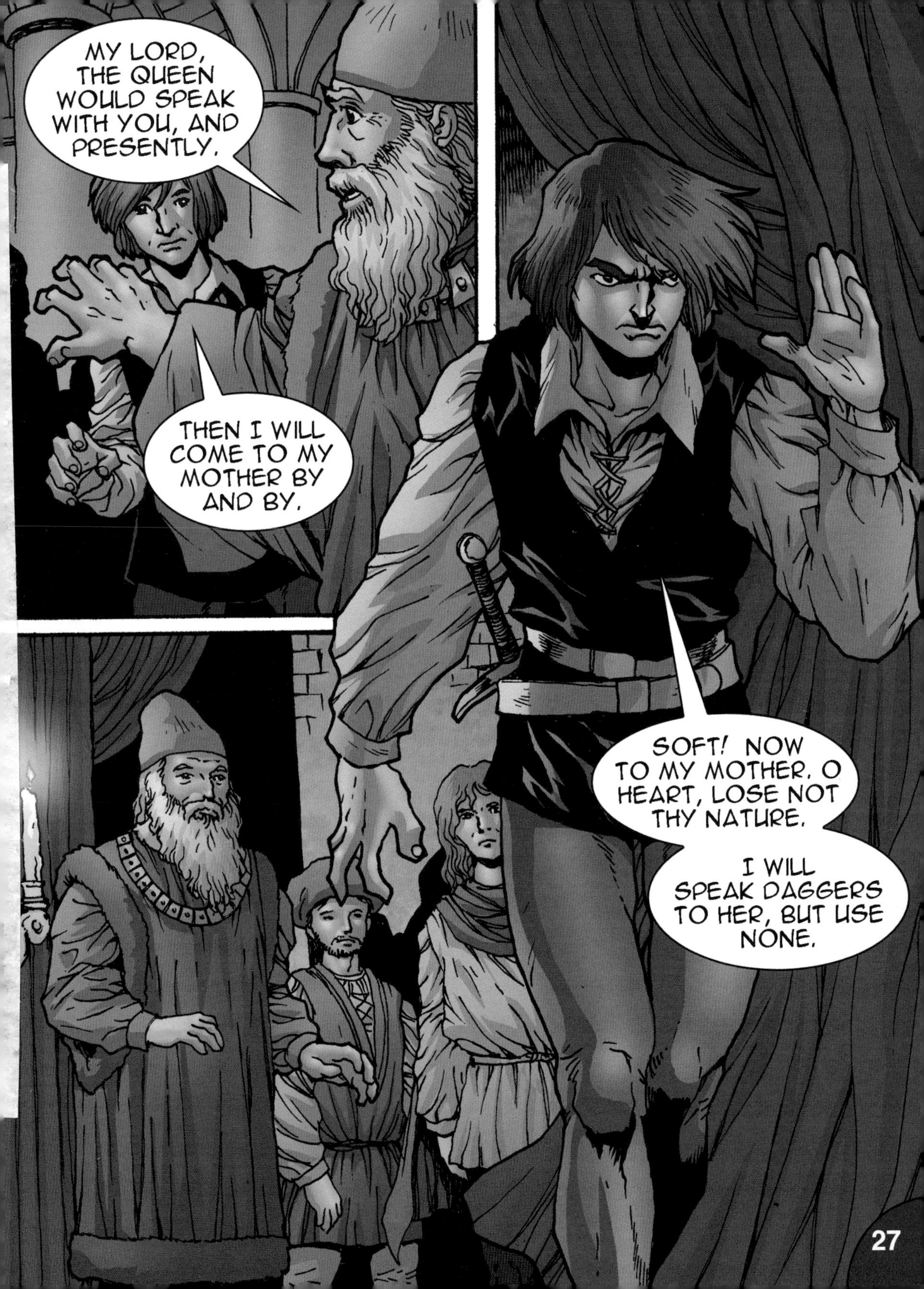
MY LORD, THE QUEEN WOULD SPEAK WITH YOU, AND PRESENTLY.
THEN I WILL COME TO MY MOTHER BY AND BY.
SOFT! NOW TO MY MOTHER. O HEART, LOSE NOT THY NATURE.
I WILL SPEAK DAGGERS TO HER, BUT USE NONE.

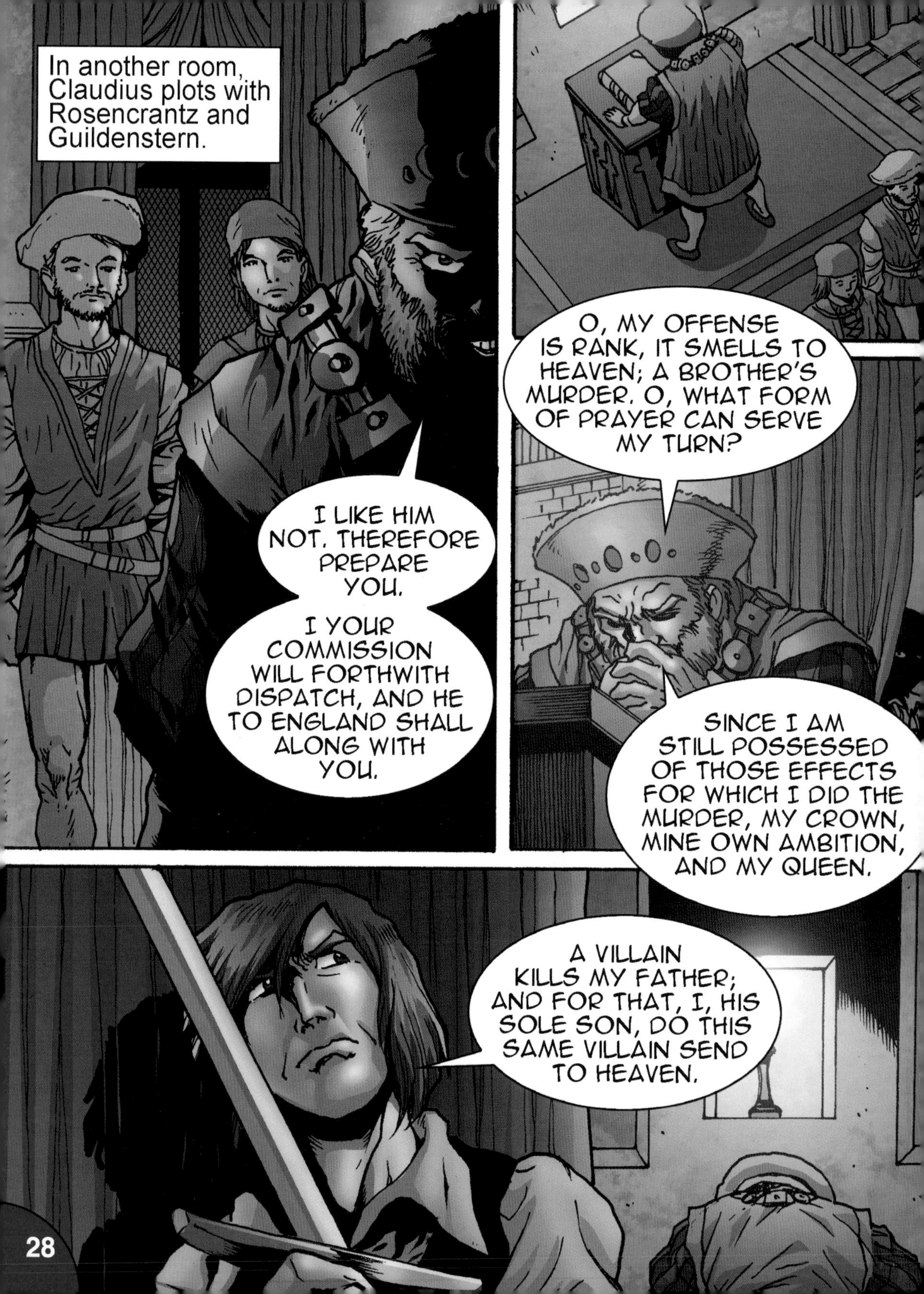
In another room, Claudius plots with Rosencrantz and Guildenstern.
I LIKE HIM NOT. THEREFORE PREPARE YOU.
I YOUR COMMISSION WILL FORTHWITH DISPATCH, AND HE TO ENGLAND SHALL ALONG WITH YOU.
O, MY OFFENSE IS RANK, IT SMELLS TO HEAVEN; A BROTHER'S MURDER. O, WHAT FORM OF PRAYER CAN SERVE MY TURN?
SINCE I AM STILL POSSESSED OF THOSE EFFECTS FOR WHICH I DID THE MURDER, MY CROWN, MINE OWN AMBITION, AND MY QUEEN.
A VILLAIN KILLS MY FATHER; AND FOR THAT, I, HIS SOLE SON, DO THIS SAME VILLAIN SEND TO HEAVEN.

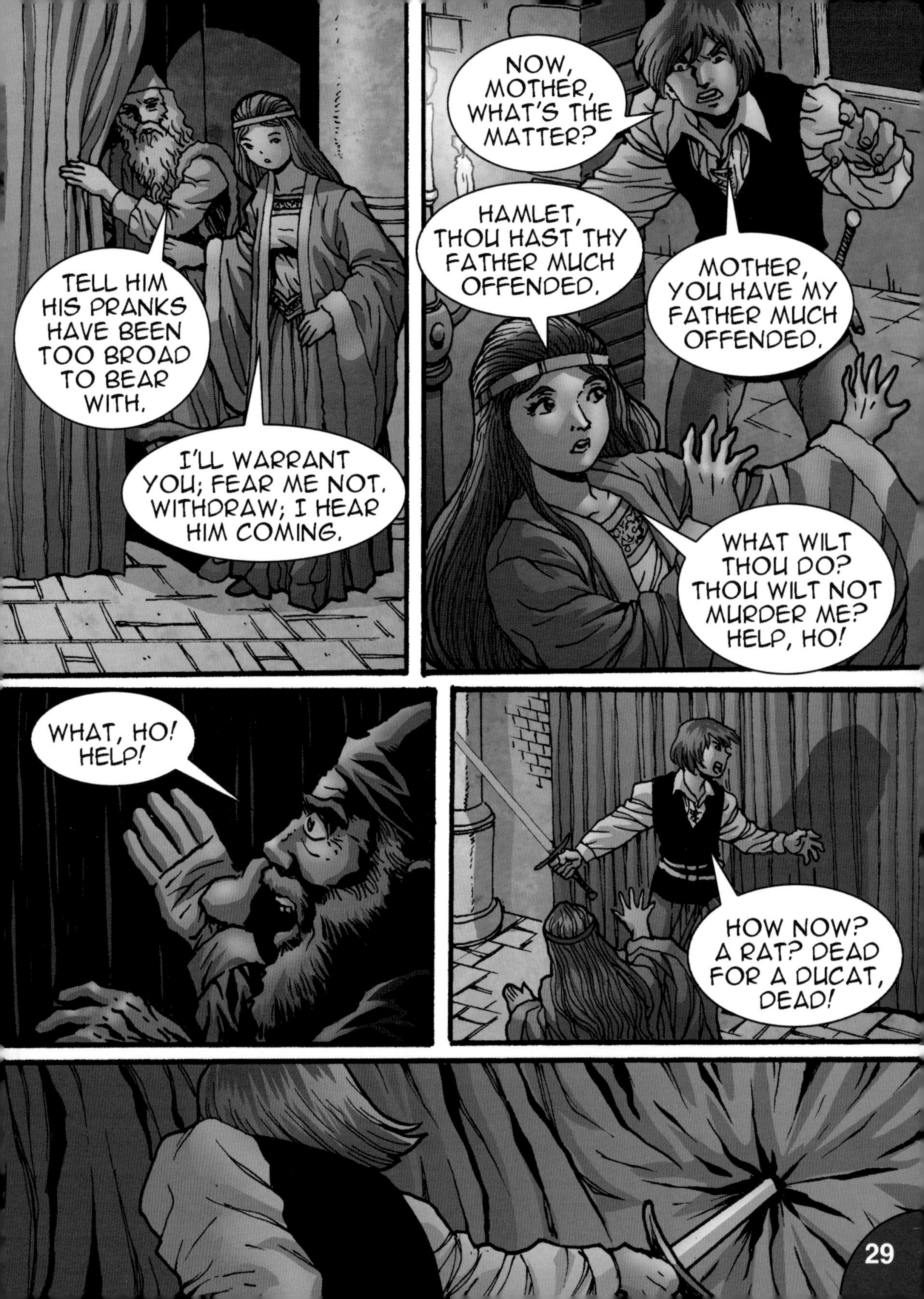
TELL HIM HIS PRANKS HAVE BEEN TOO BROAD TO BEAR WITH.
I'LL WARRANT YOU; FEAR ME NOT. WITHDRAW; I HEAR HIM COMING.
NOW, MOTHER, WHAT'S THE MATTER?
HAMLET, THOU HAST THY FATHER MUCH OFFENDED.
MOTHER, YOU HAVE MY FATHER MUCH OFFENDED.
WHAT WILT THOU DO? THOU WILT NOT MURDER ME? HELP, HO!
WHAT, HO! HELP!
HOW NOW? A RAT? DEAD FOR A DUCAT, DEAD!

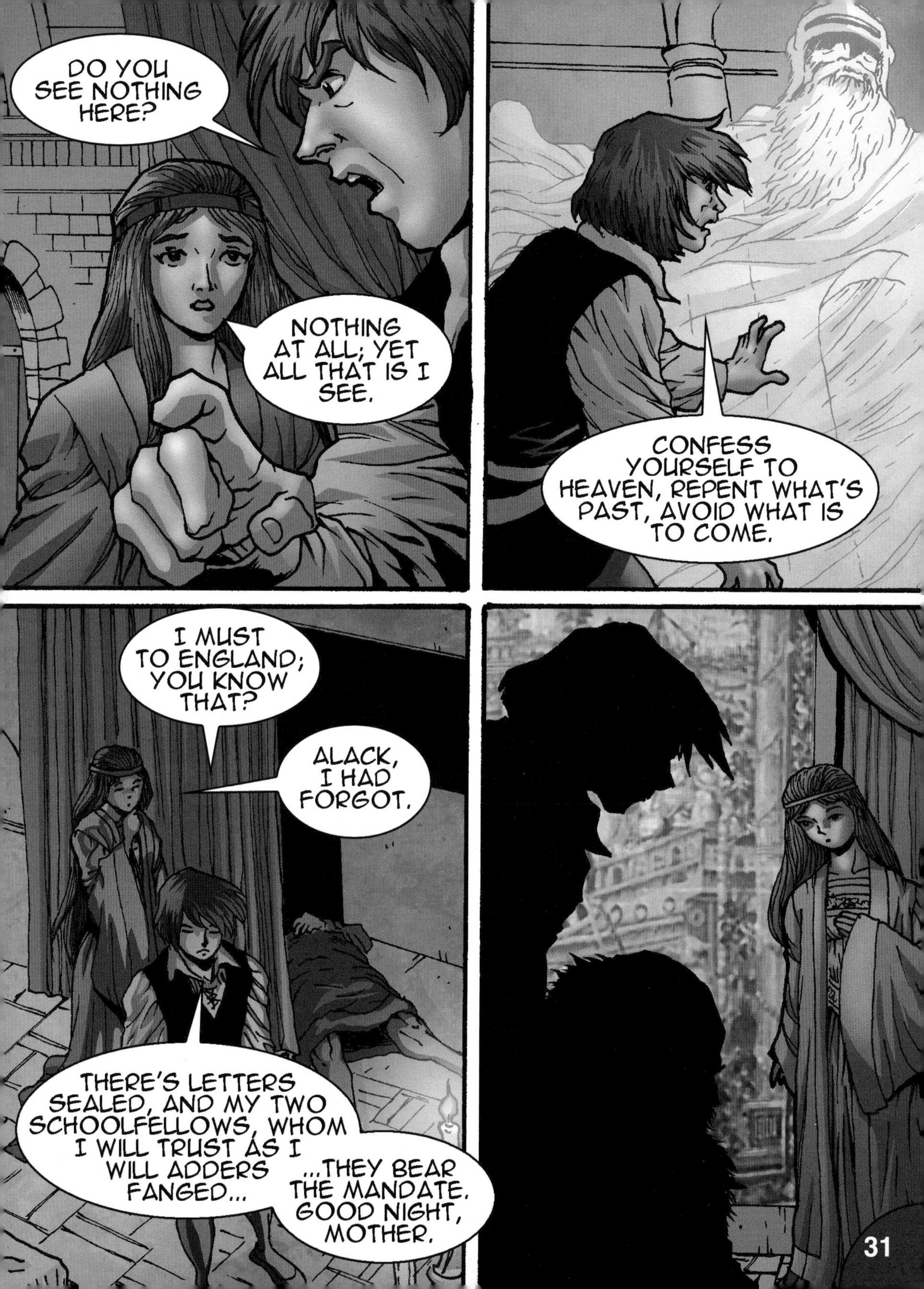
DO YOU SEE NOTHING HERE?
NOTHING AT ALL; YET ALL THAT IS I SEE.
CONFESS YOURSELF TO HEAVEN, REPENT WHAT'S PAST, AVOID WHAT IS TO COME.
I MUST TO ENGLAND; YOU KNOW THAT?
ALACK, I HAD FORGOT.
THERE'S LETTERS SEALED, AND MY TWO SCHOOLFELLOWS, WHOM I WILL TRUST AS I WILL ADDERS FANGED...
...THEY BEAR THE MANDATE. GOOD NIGHT, MOTHER.

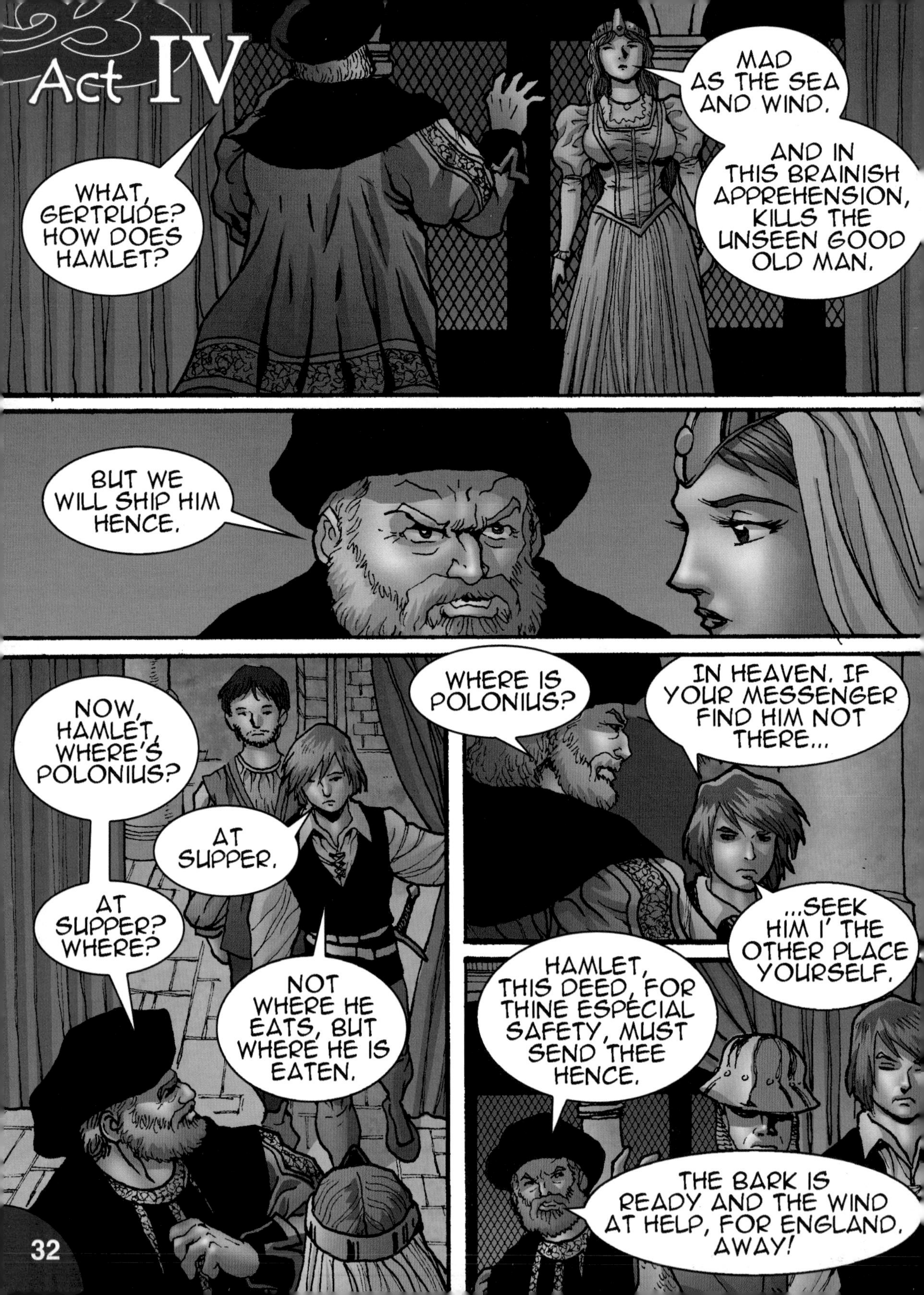
Act IV
WHAT, GERTRUDE? HOW DOES HAMLET?
MAD AS THE SEA AND WIND.
AND IN THIS BRAINISH APPREHENSION, KILLS THE UNSEEN GOOD OLD MAN.
BUT WE WILL SHIP HIM HENCE.
NOW, HAMLET, WHERE'S POLONIUS?
AT SUPPER.
AT SUPPER? WHERE?
NOT WHERE HE EATS, BUT WHERE HE IS EATEN.
WHERE IS POLONIUS?
IN HEAVEN. IF YOUR MESSENGER FIND HIM NOT THERE...
...SEEK HIM I' THE OTHER PLACE YOURSELF.
HAMLET, THIS DEED, FOR THINE ESPECIAL SAFETY, MUST SEND THEE HENCE.
THE BARK IS READY AND THE WIND AT HELP, FOR ENGLAND. AWAY!

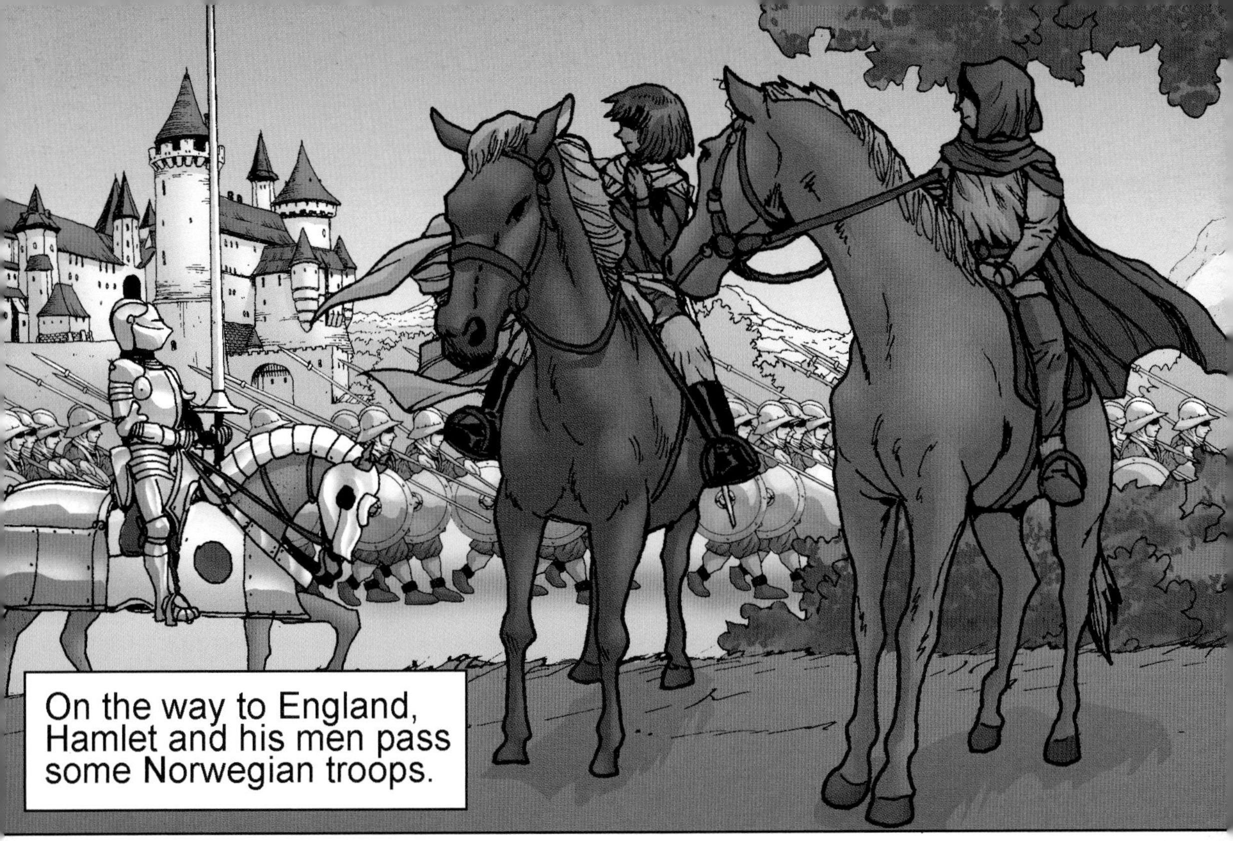
On the way to England, Hamlet and his men pass some Norwegian troops.

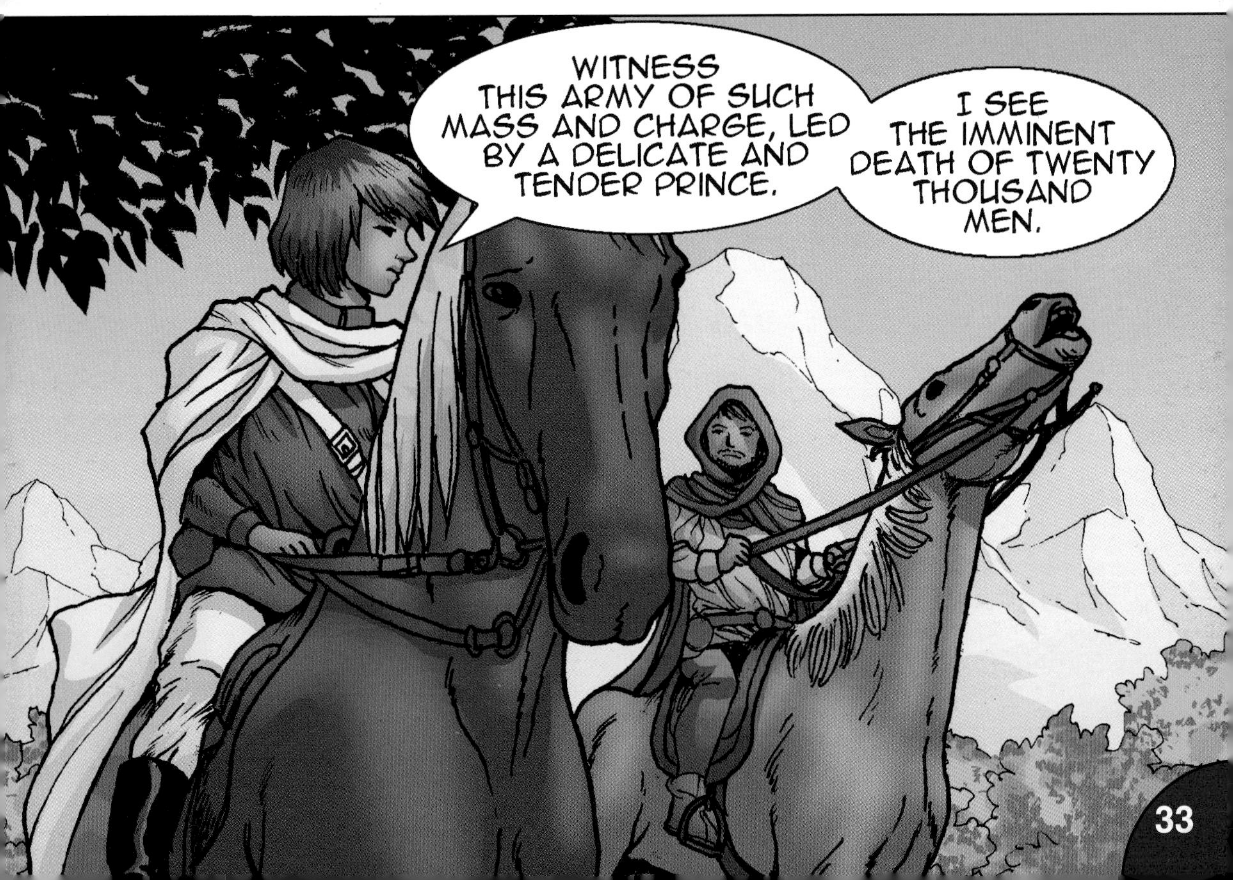
WITNESS THIS ARMY OF SUCH MASS AND CHARGE, LED BY A DELICATE AND TENDER PRINCE.
I SEE THE IMMINENT DEATH OF TWENTY THOUSAND MEN.

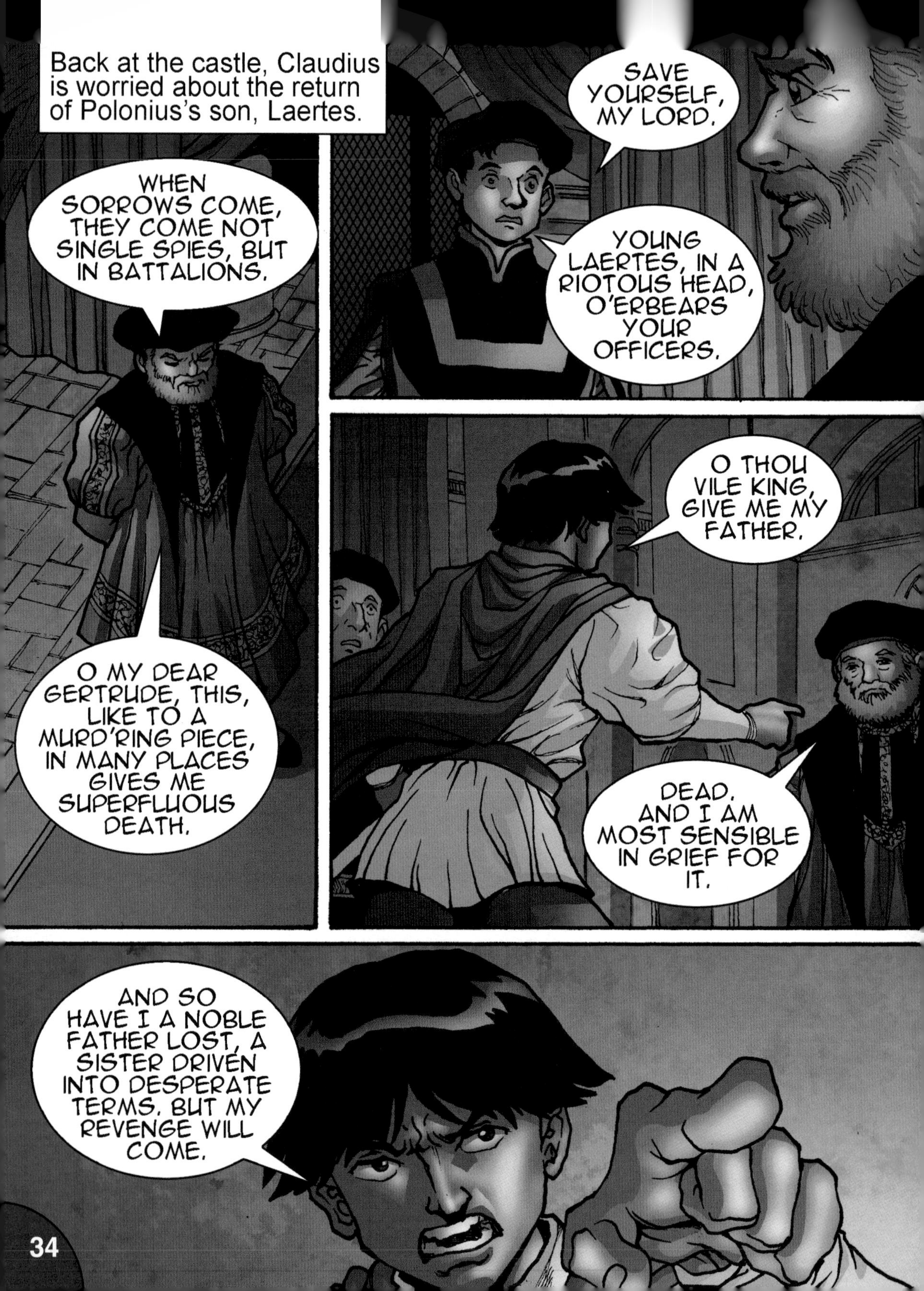
Back at the castle, Claudius is worried about the return of Polonius's son, Laertes.
WHEN SORROWS COME, THEY COME NOT SINGLE SPIES, BUT IN BATTALIONS.
O MY DEAR GERTRUDE, THIS, LIKE TO A MURD'RING PIECE, IN MANY PLACES GIVES ME SUPERFLUOUS DEATH.
SAVE YOURSELF, MY LORD.
YOUNG LAERTES, IN A RIOTOUS HEAD, O'ERBEARS YOUR OFFICERS.
O THOU VILE KING, GIVE ME MY FATHER.
DEAD. AND I AM MOST SENSIBLE IN GRIEF FOR IT.
AND SO HAVE I A NOBLE FATHER LOST, A SISTER DRIVEN INTO DESPERATE TERMS. BUT MY REVENGE WILL COME.

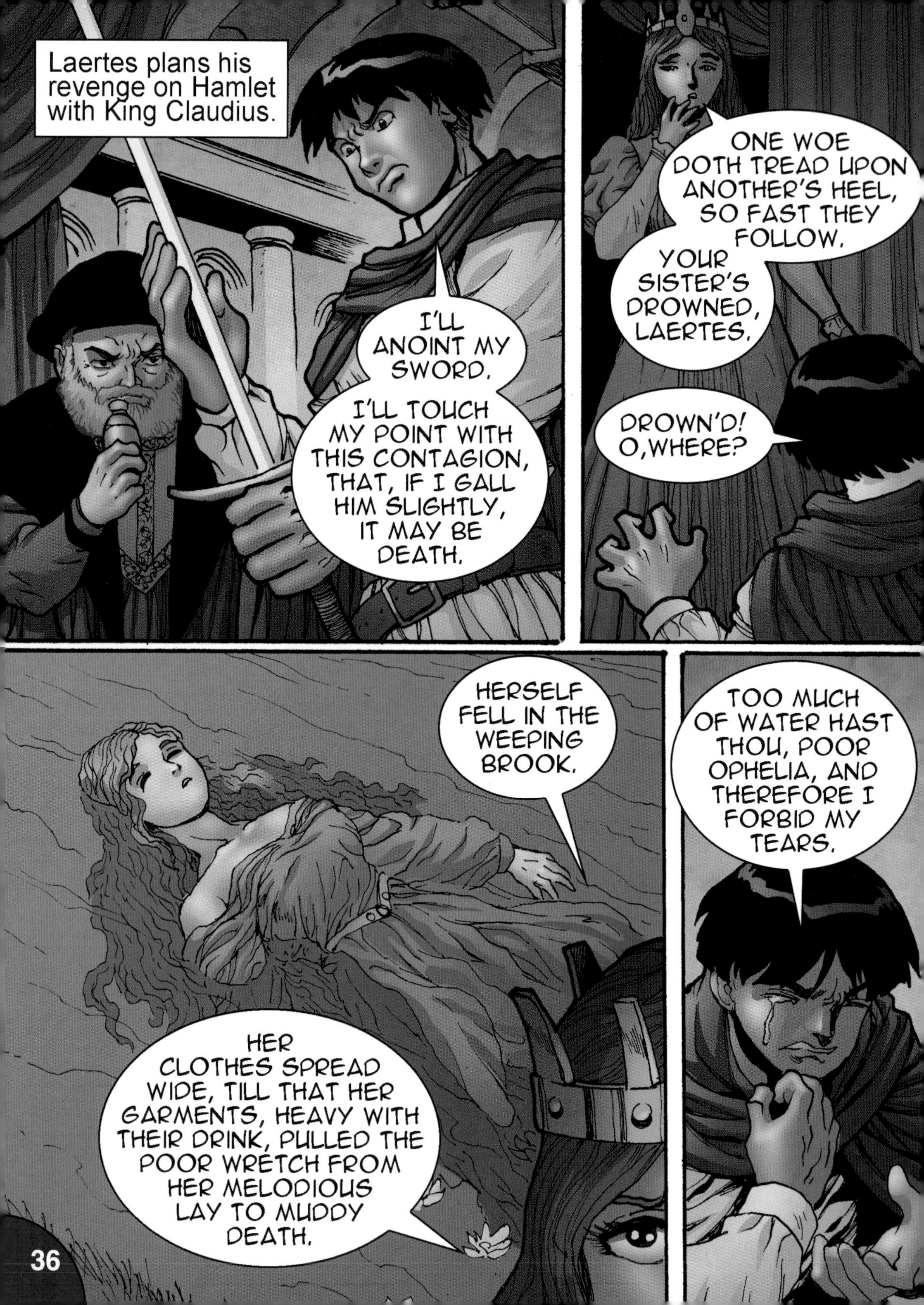
Laertes plans his revenge on Hamlet with King Claudius.
I'LL ANOINT MY SWORD.
I'LL TOUCH MY POINT WITH THIS CONTAGION, THAT, IF I GALL HIM SLIGHTLY, IT MAY BE DEATH.
ONE WOE DOTH TREAD UPON ANOTHER'S HEEL, SO FAST THEY FOLLOW.
YOUR SISTER'S DROWNED, LAERTES.
DROWN'D! O,WHERE?
HERSELF FELL IN THE WEEPING BROOK.
HER CLOTHES SPREAD WIDE, TILL THAT HER GARMENTS, HEAVY WITH THEIR DRINK, PULLED THE POOR WRETCH FROM HER MELODIOUS LAY TO MUDDY DEATH.
TOO MUCH OF WATER HAST THOU, POOR OPHELIA, AND THEREFORE I FORBID MY TEARS.

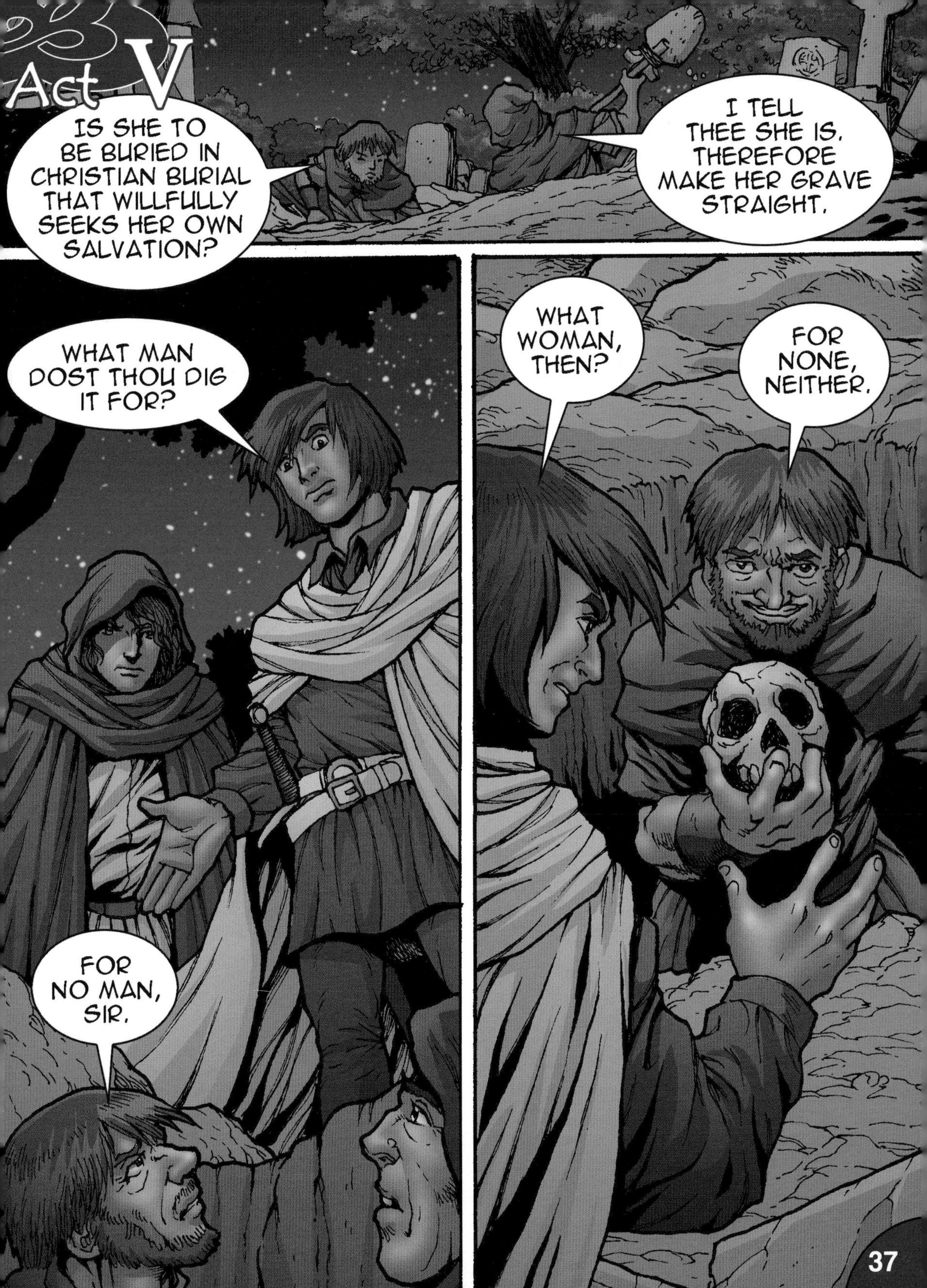
Act V
IS SHE TO BE BURIED IN CHRISTIAN BURIAL THAT WILLFULLY SEEKS HER OWN SALVATION?
I TELL THEE SHE IS. THEREFORE MAKE HER GRAVE STRAIGHT.
WHAT MAN DOST THOU DIG IT FOR?
FOR NO MAN, SIR.
WHAT WOMAN, THEN?
FOR NONE, NEITHER.

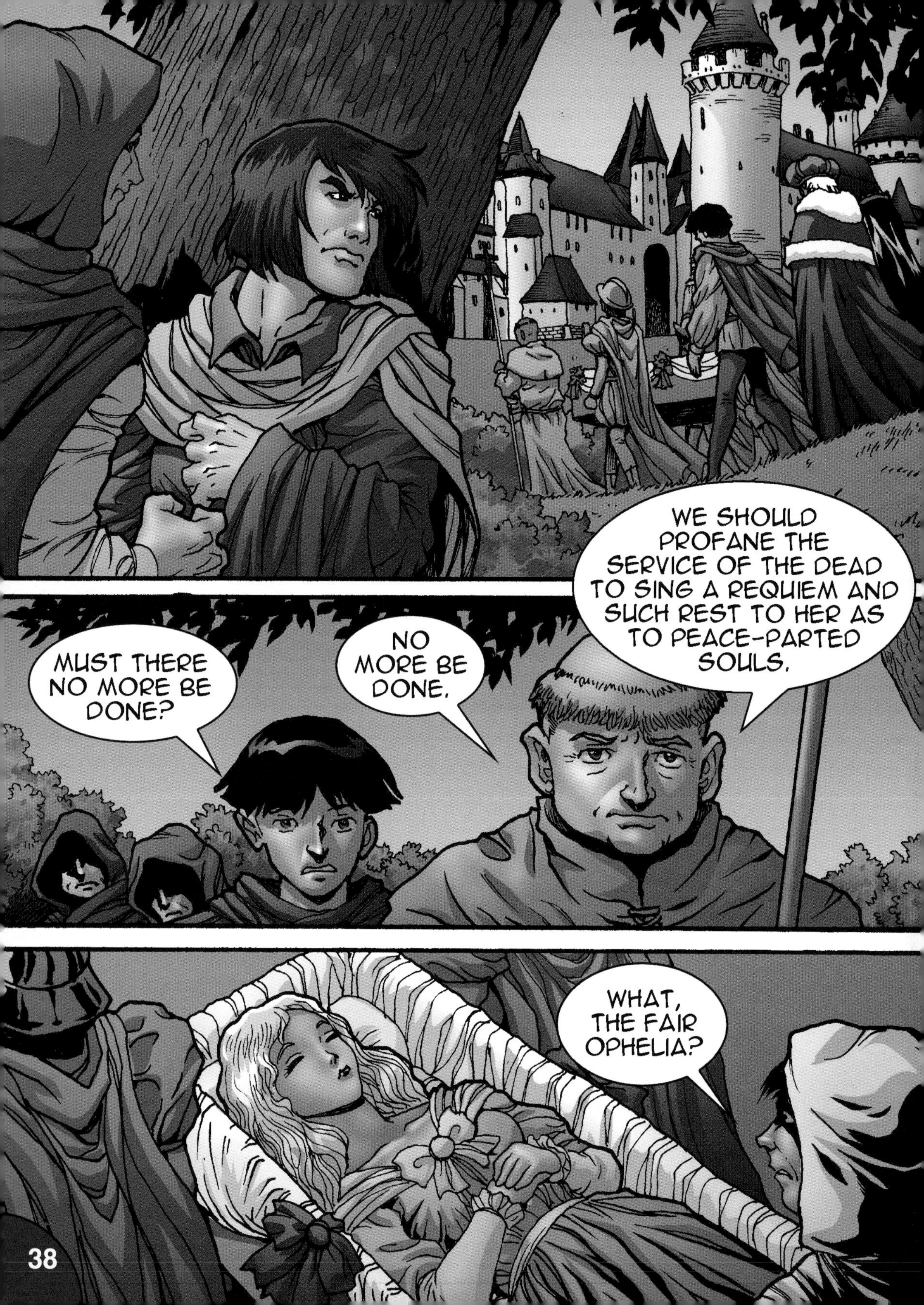
MUST THERE NO MORE BE DONE?
NO MORE BE DONE.
WE SHOULD PROFANE THE SERVICE OF THE DEAD TO SING A REQUIEM AND SUCH REST TO HER AS TO PEACE-PARTED SOULS.
WHAT, THE FAIR OPHELIA?

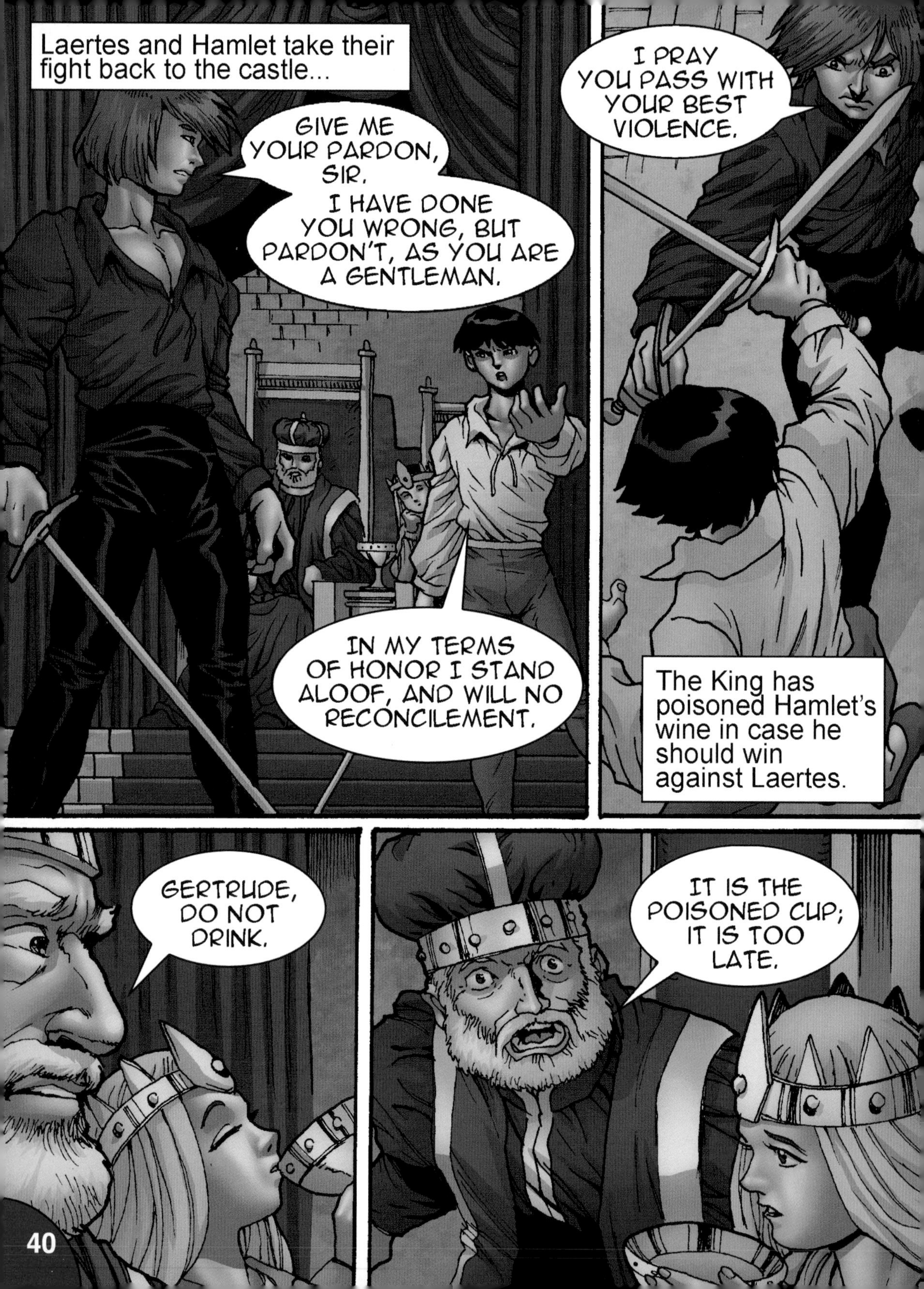
Laertes and Hamlet take their fight back to the castle...
GIVE ME YOUR PARDON, SIR.
I HAVE DONE YOU WRONG, BUT PARDON'T, AS YOU ARE A GENTLEMAN.
IN MY TERMS OF HONOR I STAND ALOOF, AND WILL NO RECONCILEMENT.
I PRAY YOU PASS WITH YOUR BEST VIOLENCE.
The King has poisoned Hamlet's wine in case he should win against Laertes.
GERTRUDE, DO NOT DRINK.
IT IS THE POISONED CUP; IT IS TOO LATE.

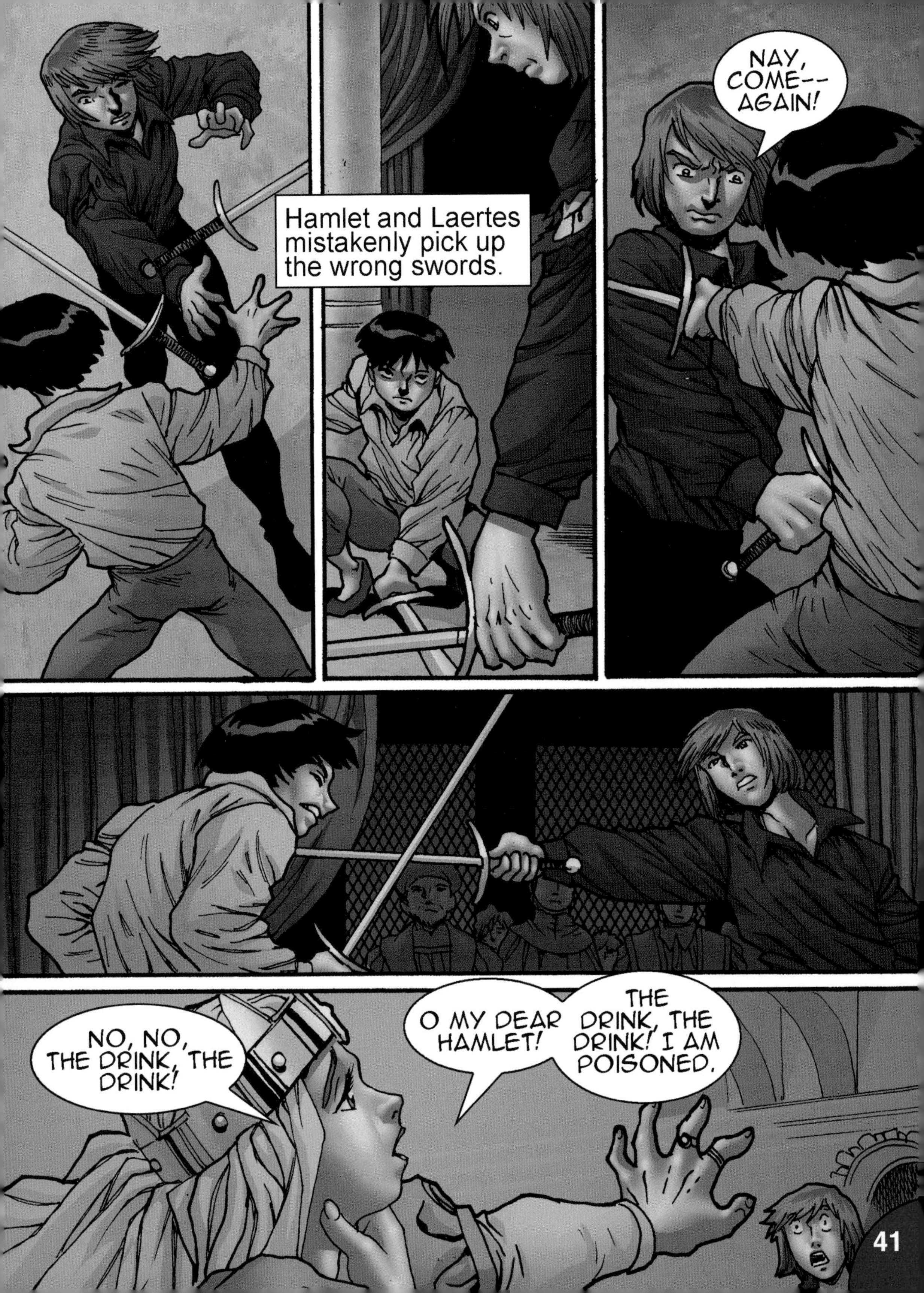
Hamlet and Laertes mistakenly pick up the wrong swords.
NAY, COME-- AGAIN!
NO, NO, THE DRINK, THE DRINK!
O MY DEAR HAMLET!
THE DRINK, THE DRINK! I AM POISONED.

42

The End 43

Hamlet was written in about 1599 to 1601. It is part of Shakespeare's *First Folio*, which was printed in 1623. The full title of the five-act revenge tragedy is *Hamlet, Prince of Denmark*.

Shakespeare based *Hamlet* on historical works by Saxo Grammaticus. Saxo was a historian who wrote the first great history of the Danish people. But Shakespeare expanded the characters and added a mystical element.

Hamlet revolves around the revenge of the murder of Hamlet's father, King Hamlet. When the play opens, Hamlet is mourning his father's death and his mother's marriage to his uncle, the new king Claudius.

The ghost of King Hamlet appears and speaks to Hamlet. He tells Hamlet that he was murdered and that Hamlet must avenge him. Hamlet pretends madness to fool Claudius, which causes Claudius to hire Hamlet's friends to spy on him. Hamlet also fools Ophelia, whom he loves.

When a group of actors arrives, Hamlet arranges for them to put on a play of his father's death. This causes King Claudius to worry. Hamlet then confronts his mother and kills Ophelia's father, Polonius, who was spying on them. After this, Hamlet is sent to England but returns when he finds out Claudius had plotted to have him killed there.

At Hamlet's return, he finds that Ophelia has died and her brother is seeking revenge for his father and sister's deaths. Claudius arranges for a poisoned drink and sword to kill Hamlet. In the end, all present are killed by poison or fighting. The Prince of Norway appears to discover the tragedy.

Since its beginning, Hamlet has been performed onstage throughout the world. There are also both film and television adaptations of this famous play.

Famous Phrases

The lady doth protest too much.

Something is rotten in the state of Denmark.

Take it to heart.

To thine own self be true.

To be, or not to be—that is the question.

When we have shuffled off this mortal coil.

About the Author

William Shakespeare was baptized on April 26, 1564, in Stratford-upon-Avon, England. At the time, records were not kept of births, however, the churches did record baptisms, weddings, and deaths. So, we know approximately when he was born. Traditionally, his birth is celebrated on April 23.

William was the son of John Shakespeare, a tradesman, and Mary Arden. He most likely attended grammar school and learned to read, write, and speak Latin.

Shakespeare did not go on to the university. Instead, he married Anne Hathaway at age 18. They had three children, Susanna, Hamnet, and Judith. Not much is known about Shakespeare's life at this time. By 1592 he had moved to London, and his name began to appear in the literary world.

In 1594, Shakespeare became an important member of Lord Chamberlain's company of players. This group had the best actors and the best theater, the Globe. For the next 20 years, Shakespeare devoted himself to writing. He died on April 23, 1616, but his works have lived on.

Additional Works by Shakespeare

The Comedy of Errors (1589–94)
The Taming of the Shrew (1590–94)
Romeo and Juliet (1594–96)
A Midsummer Night's Dream (1595–96)
Much Ado About Nothing (1598–99)
As You Like It (1598–1600)
Hamlet (1599–1601)
Twelfth Night (1600–02)
Othello (1603–04)
King Lear (1605–06)
Macbeth (1606–07)
The Tempest (1611)

About the Adapter

Ben Dunn is affectionately called the "Godfather of American Manga." He founded Antarctic Press, one of the largest comic companies in the United States. His works appear in Marvel and Image comics. He is best known for his series *Ninja High School* and *Warrior Nun Areala*.

Rebecca Dunn is a schoolteacher who enjoys both graphic novels and classic literature. She lives in the Dallas area with her husband, Ben Dunn, and their two children, Kal and Mackenzie.

Glossary

arras - a wall hanging.

bark - a small sailing ship.

choler - a feeling of anger.

confound - to confuse others.

contagion - poison.

doublet - a man's jacket.

fishmonger - a person who sells fish.

lunacy - insanity or madness.

perchance - by mere chance.

repel - repulse or push away.

requiem - a song of grief.

surmise - to form an idea based on little or no evidence.

Web Sites

To learn more about William Shakespeare, visit ABDO Publishing Company on the World Wide Web at **www.abdopublishing.com**. Web sites about Shakespeare are featured on our Book Links page. These links are routinely monitored and updated to provide the most current information available.